SLOW BURN

Into The Fire Series

J.H. CROIX

J.H. CROIX

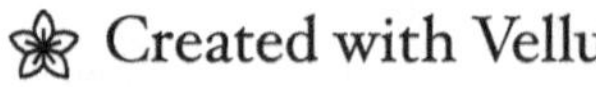 Created with Vellum

This one goes out to LM, my friend—always there in heart and soul and with lots of laughter!

Sign up for my newsletter for information on new releases & get a FREE copy of one of my books!

http://jhcroixauthor.com/subscribe/

Follow me!
jhcroix@jhcroix.com
https://amazon.com/author/jhcroix
https://www.bookbub.com/authors/j-h-croix
https://www.facebook.com/jhcroix

SLOW BURN

I put out fires for a living. I can take some heat. But Maisie drives me crazy. She's smart-mouthed, sarcastic and argumentative.

This town's too small for both of us. But she works for me. *Unfortunately*. It's a big no-no for me to want her.

She's brash and beautiful and tempts me beyond distraction. There are different kinds of fire, and this one will make her melt.

There's only one problem: this fire might be too hot for both of us.

Chapter One

MAISIE

"Let me see if I understand you. Your cat got stuck in a tree, so you used your excavator to get him out?" I asked.

"Yes, that's what I said," Carrie Dodge explained, her tone exasperated.

I only knew Carrie's name because that was the second order of business whenever I answered a call at Willow Brook Fire & Rescue. Sadly, I still wasn't clear on what the nature of Carrie's emergency was.

"So, is your cat okay?"

Carrie's sigh came through the line. "Herman is fine. It's my excavator that's the problem."

When I answered a minute ago, Carrie had spoken so quickly, all I'd been able to piece together was something to do with a tree, a cat, and an excavator.

"Tell me what happened to your excavator."

I waited to hear the excavator had a name. Because this was Alaska and people named their tools and things like that here. I'd only lived here about two years, but I'd quickly come to learn some things were more important than others. Shiny cars—not so much. Excavators or fishing gear—worth their weight in gold.

"Oh, well, it was all fine at first. I got it right up by the tree, and Herman hopped in the bucket no problem. I lowered him to the ground and when I was turning it around, I forgot how close the ditch was and it fell in. I'm stuck inside," Carrie explained.

Rather calmly, I might add. This was the first mention a human was involved in this emergency beyond the role of an observer.

I tapped the alarm button on my desk. That would alert the crew on duty while I kept Carrie on the line until they arrived at her location. I'd already linked her GPS coordinates to our system. With rapid fire typing, I filled in a summary for the crew to see.

"Are you injured?" I asked Carrie, thinking to myself as long as she was okay, it was almost funny she'd neglected to mention her predicament this far into our call. I'd started out worried about the cat, then the excavator, when lo and behold, she was trapped in an excavator that had fallen in a ditch.

"I think so," Carrie said with a sigh. "Herman's looking at me through the window. My shoulder hurts a little."

"Do you mind if I get some basic info from you while the rescue crew's headed your way?"

"I suppose not," Carrie replied with another sigh.

I heard the garage doors opening on the back of Willow Brook's Fire & Rescue building and the sirens blare. Within seconds, an ambulance was racing past the front windows with a fire truck in its wake.

Carrie was remarkably calm and gave me her information with a few huffs here and there. I sensed she was more annoyed with her situation than with me.

I heard one of the crewmembers radioing to report they were within three minutes. I was the sole dispatcher for Willow Brook Fire & Rescue. Though Willow Brook was a small town in Alaska, nestled in a valley in the foothills of the Alaska Range, its proximity to Anchorage and central location in the state had resulted in its Fire & Rescue crews being one of the hubs in the state. Two interagency hotshot crews ran out of Willow Brook, along with a local crew. All three crews were fully trained for hotshot firefighting, which required intensive training and grueling work. Hotshot teams were sent to the most dangerous, remote fires in the country. Alaska's sprawling geography lent itself to plenty of fires. The Willow Brook teams mostly served Alaska, however they went wherever they were called. When they weren't deep in the wilderness fighting wildfires, they handled whatever came up here.

I chatted with Carrie until I heard the crew arrive. As soon as I ended my call with her, my other line beeped, indicating someone from the crew was calling in.

"Yes?"

"Hey Maze, what's the emergency? The cat or the excavator?" Beck Steele asked.

The moment he spoke, I got annoyed. Beck invariably annoyed me. I could practically see him grinning. I gritted my teeth and told myself I'd stay calm and professional.

"Neither. Carrie, the woman calling, is stuck in the excavator. Aren't you there?" I asked, proud of myself for keeping my voice perfectly level.

"Not yet. Crew says she's fine by the way. Mind telling me what this has to do with a cat?"

"Her cat was in a tree. She used the excavator bucket to get him out, and then the excavator tipped into a ditch," I explained.

"Of course. Because it makes perfect sense to use an excavator to get a cat out of a tree," he said with a low chuckle, his tone dry.

No matter what, Beck managed to get under my skin. Next thing I knew, I was arguing the point.

"It's not the worst idea. I mean, she got Herman out of the tree," I countered.

"Herman?"

"The cat. His name is Herman," I explained.

Another low chuckle from Beck sent my belly into a tailspin of flutters. I was hot and prickly all over and inanely arguing about the sensibility of using an excavator to get a cat out of a tree.

"Do you need anything else from me?" I snapped.

"Nah. Nice chatting, Maze," he replied.

The line went dead in my ear. I swore he

called me like this just to piss me off. I shook my thoughts off of him, adjusted my headset and quickly entered everything from the call in our data system. I was unusually curious to see how Carrie was. Carrie's unflappable attitude got to me and made me want to know for certain she'd be okay.

I fielded a few more calls in the time the crew was out. They were still out when the top of the hour rolled around, and the call center in Anchorage took over duty for me to take a break. I still hadn't heard back from the crew and hoped Carrie was okay. I'd learned it wasn't the least bit helpful for crews to have me calling to check in, so I'd just have to wait. I powered down my computer and headed into the back area.

Two of our crews were out in the middle of freaking nowhere dealing with two different backcountry fires in Alaska. With the remaining crew out, the back of the station was deserted. I was feeling grubby after a morning changing the oil on the old truck Gram had left me. A side benefit to working at Fire & Rescue was access to the massive garage bays and tools galore. The crews handled all of their own maintenance. Amongst the three crews, there was a single female firefighter, Susannah Gilmore. She was also one of the few friends I had. Lately, she'd taught me how to change the oil in my truck, so I'd tried it this morning when no one was around. I kind of wished she wasn't out in the field because I didn't feel comfortable enough to ask any of the guys if I'd done it right.

Whether I'd changed the oil properly or not, I could use a shower. I'd been trying to figure out what to do about my broken hot water heater for over a week now. Cold showers sucked, so I'd been taking advantage of the showers here whenever I could. I preferred not to do so when anyone was around, so I planned to make it quick. The crew hadn't radioed they were on their way back yet, so I figured I had a little time.

Inside of a few minutes, I was savoring the steaming hot water pouring over me. The industrial hot water pressure here was phenomenal. I wondered if I could find a way to get this kind of pressure at Gram's house. My heart gave a little squeeze. It was technically my house because Gram had left it to me when she passed away, but I still couldn't seem to think of it as mine. It felt too much like her. I gave my head a shake and grabbed the soap, quickly soaping myself all over. I was rinsing the shampoo from my hair when I heard a voice.

"What the..."

I opened my eyes to see Beck standing in the entryway to the showers. I might've forgotten to mention Beck was the sexiest, most handsome man I'd ever known in person. There he stood in all of his glory. He still had his gear half on, but he'd taken his shirt off. His black curls were a wild mess, and he had dirt streaked on his cheeks and arms. His chest was a work of art—all glistening muscle, every inch of it practically carved from stone. His heavy-duty coveralls were hanging at his waist, tempting my eyes to look further down.

I was so stupidly staring at him, I momentarily forgot I was completely naked. Beck's eyes were wide, and his mouth hung open. He snapped it shut, and his eyes—those gorgeous, sinfully green eyes raked over me. If I didn't know better, I might've thought his gaze darkened with desire. But that was crazy, and I was naked.

Chapter Two

BECK

Maisie Rogers stood in the showers—her delectable body bare for me to see. I couldn't have kept my eyes from taking a detour along every curve if I'd wanted to. Soap bubbles ran down her skin. I wanted to be those bubbles, caressing every inch of her skin.

Holy smokes. I was stuck right where I was. Her dark brown curls were wet and fell down around her shoulders, the water almost straightening them, but they were so wild, they couldn't be tamed. Her big brown eyes were like saucers. Oh, I'd have guessed Maisie had a body to die for, but she kept it hidden behind her t-shirts and jeans. Her breasts— oh my fucking God her breasts. They were round and bouncy with dusky pink nipples. I was perhaps ten feet away from her, so I couldn't be certain, but I was pretty sure her nipples got tight as I stood there and gaped at her.

Her waist curved in and then her hips flared out. My cock was hard inside of a second. I could instantly imagine gripping those hips, the soft flesh giving way, and sinking inside of her. Suddenly, she squeaked and spun around. If she thought that would help matters, nope. Her bottom was just as delectable as the rest of her. I'd never been one to love thin women. They were too, well, thin. I liked something to hold onto. Maisie had curves for days, plenty to hold onto.

"Do you mind?" she snapped, keeping her back to me.

Her voice was muffled by the water, but her snippy attitude came through loud and clear. Whenever she got like that with me, the urge to tease her was impossible to resist.

"I don't mind at all. Not one bit," I countered, letting my words drag out.

I was speaking the plain truth. I could stand there all day and stare at her. If my cock had anything to say about it, I'd been doing a lot more than staring.

"Oh my God," she muttered. "Beck, please."

Just now, she didn't sound pissed. She sounded distressed, and it wasn't funny anymore. It suddenly occurred to me the rest of the crew would be in here any second. I didn't want anyone else to walk in on her like this. While I had always felt protective toward Maisie when she wasn't busy driving me nuts, now I felt territorial. I didn't want anyone else to see how fucking gorgeous she was.

"On my way out. I'll hold the crew at bay," I called as I forced my feet to move and walk out.

A while later, after I'd showered along with the rest of the crew, I made my way out front. I figured it would be best if Maisie and I went ahead and got the requisite awkward moment out of the way. I pushed through the swinging door out front to find her with her eyes studiously focused on her computer.

When she first started working here, she'd been pretty bitchy with the crews, but she was steady and professional on calls. So we kept her on, in part for that and in part out of loyalty to her grandmother. Carol Rogers had been our main admin person for decades. When she'd asked the police chief to hire Maisie, he'd immediately agreed. Maisie was an incredibly hard worker, and I respected her. I'd managed to keep the undercurrent of desire I felt for her at bay for a good two years now. Seeing her the way I just had wouldn't help matters.

I leaned my elbows on the counter surrounding her desk. "So Carrie Dodge is doing okay," I said, figuring if I started with something neutral and normal, perhaps it would just let us skip right past any awkwardness.

Maisie glanced up. "Oh good! You guys were there a while. What happened?"

I chuckled. "Most of the work was getting the excavator in a safe position so we could get Carrie out. She broke her collarbone and her elbow, so they transported her to the hospital. I'm still not sure how she pulled it off, but that damn excavator was on its side. If she hadn't been inside, it would've been no biggie, but she was pinned in the corner of the cab, so we had to be careful. Took some finagling."

Maisie grinned. "You shoulda heard her when she called. She didn't even mention she was in the excavator until a few minutes in."

"Doesn't surprise me a bit. Carrie's used to taking care of things herself. She was more pissed off she needed help than anything else."

"Well, I'm glad she's okay."

After that, Maisie looked back at her computer and fiddled with a bracelet on her wrist. Her teeth caught her bottom lip, worrying it. *Oh fuck. My grand plan to breeze past this went up in smoke. Two years of trying to ignore my body's draw to Maisie and now I knew exactly how she looked— every glorious fucking inch of her.*

"Didn't mean to surprise you back there. What the hell do you need to shower here for anyway?" There my mouth went, stumbling into the one topic I preferred to avoid.

Her cheeks got pink, and she kept her eyes trained on her computer screen. "My hot water heater broke," she mumbled.

Perfect. Something else to focus on other than Maisie naked and my hard cock.

"Well, why don't you get it fixed?" I asked the rather obvious question.

Her big brown eyes swung up to mine again. *Damn. She was beautiful, and she appeared to have no idea. She had these wild brown curls she barely managed to keep tucked back in a ponytail paired with wide brown eyes and thick lashes that brushed against her cheeks. Her fair skin was scattered with freckles.*

"I wasn't sure who to ask," she finally said.

"Come on, Maisie. Every one of us here

would be glad to help. How about I stop by tomorrow? I'll take a look and see if I can figure out what's wrong. If not, I'll help you install a new one."

She worried that bottom lip with her slightly crooked teeth, just crooked enough to make her smile downright endearing when she chose to let you see it.

"I'm worried it'll cost too much," she finally said.

Ah. I got it. Maisie was coasting by on what she earned, and I doubted she had any savings to speak of. Far as I knew, she was all alone since her grandmother passed away. My heart gave a funny thump. I ignored it.

"Let's start with seeing if I can fix it, okay?"

She met my eyes, her cheeks still pink, and finally nodded. "Okay."

I pushed off the counter and started to walk outside, her voice catching me right before I stepped through the door.

"Beck?"

I glanced back.

"Thank you," she said.

That's all she said, but she added a smile. It was all I could do not to turn around, walk straight to her and kiss her.

Chapter Three

MAISIE

I wiped off the kitchen counter and hung the towel over the oven handle before glancing around. Gram's kitchen was bright and airy and flowed into a living room with a breathtaking view of Swan Lake and Denali in the distance. Denali was the centerpiece of Alaska and the tallest mountain peak in North America. Gram had this home built to take full advantage of the natural beauty surrounding it. The kitchen and living room area faced the view of the lake and mountains with floor to ceiling windows stretching up to the second floor. A balcony sat against the back wall with a short hallway that contained doorways to two bedrooms and a bathroom.

Even in the short days of winter, the windows let in every bit of sun available.

The kitchen had a curved island separating it from the living room with a sage green granite countertop and updated stainless steel appliances. The light birch flooring provided additional brightness to the space with splashes of color in the multicolored rugs scattered about the living room. Everything here was Gram's. She'd updated this home only a few years before she passed away, so it felt modern and new. The outside was cedar siding with a deck that wrapped around three sides of the house. I could sit outside and look at the lake in front, stare out over the field to one side of the house with its flowers, or look into the evergreen forest on the other side.

This was the nicest place I had ever lived. By far. I had nothing but good memories of coming here to visit when I was growing up. My mom had passed away after a heart attack when I was only three years old. She'd had an undiagnosed congenital defect in one of her valves. My dad was a happenstance kind of dad. It so happened he was a dad, but that was about it. I don't know why he hadn't just turned me over to Gram, but he never did. He lugged me around like an afterthought instead. We never lived anywhere more than a year. By the time I hit high school, I stopped trying too hard to make friends because it wasn't worth it.

Fast forward to now. Gram had died and left me everything she owned two years ago. Since my mom had been her only daughter, I was her sole living relative. Even though I'd only gotten to see Gram every few years, she'd been the touchstone in my life. When I'd heard she was sick, I'd scrabbled together every penny I had to catch a flight from California to Alaska. I'd had a few weeks with her while she received hospice care before she passed away. I'd come here solely to see Gram. I had no plan and no money left when she died.

I'd been shocked to learn she'd left me everything. Everything consisted of this home and the ten acres surrounding it, a truck, a car, all the equipment in the garage and everything in the house. I also inherited another fifty acres that were in a protected preserve and to remain undeveloped forever as far as I understood. I'd been advised by Gram's estate attorney that she'd also set up a trust fund for me, but I couldn't access anything in it until I was thirty-five. I could've cared less about that mysterious trust fund.

The afternoon I'd learned all of this had been jaw-dropping. I'd gone into that attorney's office, dragged by the police chief, Rex Masters, and Janet James, both friends of Gram. I'd been broke and with nowhere to go because I didn't have enough money to fly back to California. I'd left within an hour with more than I'd ever imagined. To top it all off, Chief Masters had offered me Gram's old job at the Fire & Rescue station. To this day, I was pretty sure Gram had asked him to, but I didn't mind. I'd needed a job. Badly.

By some miracle, I'd kept my grades up in school and had snagged a scholarship to a local college. Before coming here, I'd managed to graduate with a degree in biology and had been working my butt off at a local coffee shop while I took one class per semester to work toward becoming an EMT. Coffee shop pay wasn't much. I didn't make a ton as a dispatch operator, but it was a steady schedule and I had benefits. This job had turned out to be the perfect fit for me. My life now was more stable than it had ever been.

I looked around Gram's home and wondered how Beck would see it. Just thinking about Beck made me hot all over. I'd thought I might actually die of embarrassment when he straight out asked why I was showering at the station. I'd been hoping we could pretend he'd never seen me bare ass naked. Then he'd gone and offered to come help with the hot water heater.

I hadn't quite figured out how to *be* here in Willow Brook. I was used to being the odd one out and relying solely on myself. Always minding my own business, never around long enough for anyone to care too much. Here, everyone knew Gram. Even though they barely knew me, they acted like I was their long-lost relative. It was sort of weird for me. I knew they meant to be nice, but I wasn't used to it and didn't feel like I'd earned it.

My eyes landed on the clock, a whimsical clock with a bold, black raven as a backdrop and a raven's call when the clock struck the hour. Oh shit. Beck would be here any minute.

Calm down, girl. He's just here to fix your hot water heater.

Uh yeah, but he saw me naked. Totally naked.

And OMG, he's hot.

I hadn't forgotten the sight of his bare chest. Hell, I'd been fantasizing about his chest ever since I'd seen it yesterday. I could seriously go for a chance to have every hard inch of him plastered to me. Heat pooled in my belly just thinking about it. Oh shit. I needed to get it together. Beck would never go for me. He was way out of my league. My God, he was hot guy calendar material. I was just me, a normal looking girl.

I needed to stop getting all hot and bothered over him. He was nice and all, but he was a flirt. I knew his reputation. He loved summer because he could date a new woman every week with the tourists flocking here. As far as I could tell, he did.

I mentally shook myself. Thinking about Beck in any way other than just as a guy I worked with was a bad idea. Technically, he was one of my bosses. Chief Masters and the three crew superintendents were the ones who ran the show at Willow Brook Fire & Rescue. The only reason he was here was to help me with the hot water heater. That was it. I really wanted my hot water back. Though I had everything I needed, I didn't have much money saved up, so I'd been worrying about what to do.

A sharp knock nudged me out of my thoughts. I spun around and hurried to the kitchen door. Opening it, my breath caught the second I saw Beck. His rumpled black curls glinted in the bright, late afternoon sun. His green eyes crinkled at the corners with his perpetually flirtatious grin. He bandied that grin about quite liberally, so I never assumed it was meant for me. Beck would probably flirt with a rock if given the chance.

"Hey Maze," he said as he stepped past me.

He was the only person who used that nickname with me. I simultaneously hated it and loved it.

My eyes landed on his motorcycle, the sun glinting off the handlebars. His bike suited his personality—simple and black, it had clearly seen a lot of action. No vanity bike for him.

Beck wore a faded navy t-shirt paired with black jeans and battered leather boots. His hardened muscles were easily visible. He was the kind of guy who had a body to die for, yet it wasn't the result of vanity. It was because that's who he was and how he lived. Hotshot firefighters were the toughest of the tough. The job demanded they stay in peak physical condition at all times. It was a matter of life or death when they were out in the backcountry, reliant on themselves and their crew to handle grueling conditions and physically brutal work for days on end.

He rested his hip against the counter, a canvas tool bag held loosely in his hand. He glanced around, his grin fading. "Damn, haven't been here since Carol was alive. It looks exactly the same," he murmured, his eyes making their way back to me.

I swallowed and tried not to flush. God, it was ridiculous how easily he affected me. My belly executed a slow flip when his eyes caught mine. Somehow, the fact he'd seen me completely naked made everything feel too close for comfort. I wasn't a prude, but it irked me to no end it had happened to be Beck who caught me in the showers. Any of the other guys, I might've been embarrassed, but I'd have gotten past it quickly. It was only Beck who got under my skin like this.

I managed a nod when he kept looking at me. "Yeah, I haven't really changed anything. No reason to."

He was quiet for a beat and then shrugged one shoulder. "Suppose not. You miss her?"

His question took me off guard, but I was nodding before I thought about it. "Yeah, yeah. I do."

He stayed quiet, his gaze somber. I tried to think if I'd ever seen Beck not teasing. I didn't think I had.

"I'm sorry," he finally said. "Sucks to lose someone who means a lot. Carol was pretty much a grandmother to all of us at the station. I know I miss her."

I'd heard many variations of this comment from a lot of the guys at the station. It made me proud and sad at once—proud to know she'd made such an impact on so many lives and sad I hadn't been able to spend more time with her. It was a plain fact that everyone who'd been in her circle in Willow Brook had seen far more of her than I ever had.

The vagaries of chance had landed my mother in the path of my footloose and fancy free father. I could only imagine how she must've been drawn to him. She'd only been eighteen years old—young and looking to spread her wings beyond the small world of Willow Brook. I'd never seen him as anything other than an irresponsible, rather childish, man. Yet, I'd watched so many women spin through his life—all of them easily seduced by his charm and way of casting this spell as if though his life was somehow glamorous. In short, my mom fell in lust or love and then died far away from Willow Brook. That left me with my dad. I'd have sold my soul for more time with Gram, but at least I'd had a few weeks with her before she died. I doubted she could ever have guessed what a gift it had been to leave me her house. If only because I'd never had a place to anchor me somewhere and now I did. She'd always been the person I considered my touchstone and now her place was my place.

I didn't realize I was just standing there, thoughts about Gram tumbling through my mind. Beck cleared his throat. I whipped my eyes back to his, momentarily startled at the understanding contained in his gaze. I had to nudge myself to recall what he'd last said.

"Yeah, I bet. A lot of the guys at the station say that. I don't quite have the grandmotherly air."

He flashed a wry grin. "Nah, but it would be kinda weird if you did. We like you just how you are. You keep us on our toes, and you do make some mean brownies. If Carol were still here, I'd have to tell her yours are better."

I couldn't help but laugh. Somehow, he'd managed to perfectly lighten the moment. He couldn't know that missing Gram wasn't as simple as just missing her for me. I couldn't think about her without all the rest of my baggage getting chucked right to the front of my mind.

"Okay, let me take a look at that hot water heater," Beck said, pushing his hip off the counter and strolling to the center of the kitchen.

"Okay, it's back here," I said, walking past him to the door at the back of the kitchen.

A half-bath and the laundry were in here, along with the currently useless hot water heater. He stepped past me and promptly started fiddling with things on the hot water heater. The bathroom was on the small side, if only because the washer and dryer, along with the hot water heater, took up what little extra space there was. Though it felt crowded and I was acutely aware of Beck's presence with my pulse humming along and flutters dancing about in my belly, I wanted to watch and see what he did. If he managed to fix it, then I'd know how to fix it myself if this happened again.

After a few minutes, he glanced over his shoulder, flashing me a grin. Dear God. He needed not to grin. It made my body go crazy. Case in point, inside of a millisecond, I was hot all over and knew my cheeks were pink. For about the thousandth time ever since I'd met Beck, I wished I didn't blush so easy.

"Easy fix," he announced before leaning back on his heels and reaching for the tool bag.

Even though my body was doing the same

crazy dance it always did when I was near Beck, I was determined to know what was wrong. "What is it?" I asked, kneeling down beside him and watching what he was doing.

"Heating element burned out. Brought one with me," he said as he grabbed something out of his bag.

He moved quickly. If I wanted to see, I'd have to look over his shoulder, which meant getting way too close for comfort. I straightened and leaned against the wall—annoyed with myself for being so ridiculous whenever I was around him.

"You seem worried, Maisie," Beck commented conversationally as he did whatever he was doing. "What're you worrying about? You'll have hot water within the hour."

"I was trying to see what you were doing, so I could fix it myself if it happened again," I said, surprising myself by stating the simple truth. I didn't like to cop to how hard I worked to rely solely on myself.

He finished whatever he was doing and closed the side panel on the hot water heater. As he stood, he tucked his tools in his bag and tossed the packaging from whatever 'element' he'd mentioned into the trash by the sink. He looked to me. The bathroom went from feeling small to crowded. His presence was so, well, large. He was all man, emanating it through his pores practically.

His deep green eyes scanned my face. "If your hot water heater breaks again, I'll fix it again," he said simply.

Why, oh why, did my pulse gallop ever faster at that comment? I tried so hard never to need anyone because, well, life had taught me that wasn't generally a good plan. There was this part of me, one I'd never known existed until just now, that thrilled to the idea Beck would be there for me if I needed him. Even if it was only for a hot water heater. It said something about the man that such a small thing turned me on. Big time.

Chapter Four

BECK

Maisie worried her bottom lip. Hell. She looked all flustered and worried and damn if I didn't want to do something ridiculous like hug her. Well, I also wanted to fuck her and had hardly been able to stop thinking about her hot naked body with soap all over it.

She was leaning against the wall in the bathroom, her tempestuous curls pulled up into a ponytail. Her cheeks were flushed pink and those wide brown eyes were wider than usual. I wasn't used to getting so rattled by a woman, I felt out of control. Take now, for example. Thank fuck I had a tool bag in hand to use to shield my hard cock. I could feel it pressing against the zipper of my jeans.

I was here for one reason only—to fix her

hot water heater. I'd done that and should now be moving right along. Instead, I was hyper aware that this was the first time I'd been truly alone with Maisie. Sure, I had moments around the station when others weren't right there with us, but someone was always nearby. Even when I saw her glorious, delectable, and hot as sin body naked in the showers yesterday, the rest of my crew was just in the other room.

Right now though, it was just Maisie and me. She was wearing a gray t-shirt with a bright purple flower on it and these swingy black cotton pants. Nothing special really. But this was Maisie and she had curves for days, curves I knew with precision in my mind's eye now. Her breasts stretched the t-shirt tight, and her lush hips filled out those cotton pants. I wanted to grab the cotton cord dangling at her waist and reel her to me.

My body was ahead of my brain because next thing I knew, that's what I'd done. My tool bag thumped to the floor as I caught that thin cotton cord and pulled her close. I didn't have to tug far as there wasn't much space to speak of in here.

Her breath came out in a little puff, her eyes widened, and her cheeks flushed cherry red. Oh, this was perfect. Inside of a second, her curves were pressed against me. I don't think I'd quite realized how long I'd wanted to feel her because I almost groaned when she bumped against me. It was a soft bump and those curves—have I mentioned how long I'd fantasized about her curves?—gave easily. She was all soft give against me. There was nothing soft about me, and most certainly not my cock right now. The feel of her sent another shot of blood straight to my groin.

"Ah, there," I murmured. "Just where I want you."

My tone came out teasing, and it was, but underneath, I was dead serious. Two years of being tortured seeing her almost every day. The sight of her naked yesterday had sent me over the edge.

"Beck, what are you doing?" she asked in a fierce whisper.

If she wanted to shove me away, she didn't even try. Her pulse fluttered in her neck. I wasn't thinking too much, not with my smart brain that is. Instead, I let my eyes drift over her face. She had these tiny freckles scattered randomly over her cheeks and nose. Her thick curly lashes brushed against her cheeks.

"Mmm, something I've wanted to do for a long time," I murmured, unwinding my hand from the cord to her waistband and sliding my palm in a slow pass down her spine.

Another small huff of her breath, and her eyes narrowed. Oh good. Don't ask me why, but Maisie getting annoyed revved my engine. I fucking loved it.

"Beck, this is..."

Her words ended with a gasp when I dipped my head and finally gave into the urge to taste her. The skin on her neck was flushed and so tempting, I had to drop a few kisses there. Then, I just had to find my way up to her mouth the millisecond she moaned.

Her mouth was as delectable as I'd imagined—plump lips that gave way the second I fit my mouth over hers. I lost all sense of anything beyond the feel of her in my arms, all lush curves against me.

She tensed for a flash before softening against me and moaning in my mouth. I backed her against the wall as need roared through me. Hot damn, she felt good. She didn't hold back, but then I wouldn't have expected her to. Maisie was a bold, opinionated woman. She drove me crazy with her tendency to argue over small points at work, but right now, she could be as brash as she liked.

Our kiss went from a flash point of contact to hot, wet and wild. Her tongue warred with mine and damn if her hands didn't start taking stock of me. I barely noticed it because I was plenty busy on my own. I did what I'd wanted to do for too damn long and cupped my palm over her bottom, pulling her hard against me. Her bottom, so round and saucy, felt amazingly good in my hand. I groaned in her mouth when she rolled her hips against me. This was too fucking perfect and better than I could've imagined.

I couldn't resist sliding my free hand over the soft curve of her belly to cup one of her breasts—full and soft, it was heavy in my hand. Her nipples were tight little points. I rolled one between my fingers and grinned against her lips when she moaned. I shoved her shirt up because I *needed*—to the point of madness—to feel her skin. It was warm under my touch. When I trailed my lips back down her neck, goose bumps rose in the wake of my touch, and she shivered against me, her breath coming out in a rough shudder.

I ground my cock into the apex of her thighs because I was close to the breaking point. This woman had driven me completely mad—in more ways than one—for two damn long years. Seeing her bare ass naked yesterday had snapped the tether on my control. I lifted my lips from her neck because I needed to see her. With her shirt shoved up, I was startled to find she had on a sheer black lace bra. Her nipples were taut against the lace. I took in the flare of her hips, the soft curve of her belly and her round, perfect breasts, my mouth practically watering at the sight.

Meanwhile, my cock was so hard, it ached. I flicked my eyes up to find hers on me—wide, dark and pooled with desire. The air around us felt heavy. Her cheeks were flushed and her breath came in rough heaves.

She gave her head a shake, closing her eyes briefly. They snapped open, and she glared at me.

"What are you doing?" she asked, her voice husky.

I sensed she was trying to find her bitchy side. Trust me when I tell you, when Maisie wanted to be a bitch, she excelled at it.

"Kissing you. Don't even try to tell me you're not enjoying it," I countered quickly.

I wasn't about to clue her in to how off kilter I was, but I could always fall back on teasing. I had that down to a science.

Her eyes narrowed. She started to say something and then snapped her mouth shut, her lips tightening in a mutinous line.

She took a deep breath. Fucking perfect.

That pushed her breasts right up against my chest. Her nipples were still tight, and I gave the one between my fingers a light squeeze.

She moved quickly, giving me a little shove and shimmying out from between the wall and me. Flouncing through the door, she yanked her shirt down, but I still got to enjoy the sight of her bottom swinging with each step. Not giving a damn if she noticed my cock was rock hard inside my jeans, I snagged my tool bag and followed her.

She stood in the center of the kitchen with her arms crossed tightly and her eyes snapping. "That shouldn't have happened," she announced, her tone sharp.

The more annoyed she was, the more I wanted to tease. Maisie made me downright contrary in the best possible way.

I leaned a hand on the island counter and arched a brow. "Why not? Don't you dare tell me you didn't like it," I said with a wink.

She tightened her arms and tapped the toe of her tennis shoe on the floor.

"Fine. It was just a kiss. Don't be all cocky about what a great kisser you are," she retorted, her tone defensive.

I stared at her, my quick comeback on the tip of my tongue. I meant to tell her I knew what a great kisser I was. Hell, I'd turned kissing into an art form. I loved women and loved having a little fun. I knew one thing women loved was a damn good kiss. I was no quickie kind of guy. Nope. I pulled out all the stops to make sure every woman I was with walked away entirely satisfied.

But my quick comeback didn't happen because my heart did this funny thing when I saw the look in Maisie's eyes. She looked worried and embarrassed, but she was trying so hard to hide it. My heart clenched and damn if I didn't want to hug her all over again. What was it with me and wanting to hug Maisie? I was definitely not accustomed to this protectiveness, this need to comfort that only Maisie elicited from me.

"Hey, I'm just teasing. You know that right?" I asked, my voice coming out gruff as I swallowed past the tight feeling in my chest.

Her eyes were bright and shiny, and for a flash, I wondered if I saw tears there. That couldn't be, so I ignored the thought.

She nodded quickly. "I know. You always tease. Everything's a joke for you. That's why that shouldn't have happened. You're sort of my boss, and I need my job. I'm not like those girls you date all the time. I won't be just passing through town. So I won't be ridiculous and pretend I didn't enjoy that kiss, but don't toy with me. Okay?"

She was completely serious, her eyes almost pleading with me. I suddenly felt awful, but I was confused as hell. It should've been easy for me to nod along and promise her it would never happen again. Problem was, all I could think about was what she would feel like naked against me.

I stared at her and willed my mind to behave. I wanted to tease because that's how I handled everything uncomfortable. But I knew that would be a really bad idea right now.

"Right. I get it. I wasn't trying to toy with you. For the record, I'm not an ass, you know?"

"I know you're not. Just..." She paused and bit her lip. "Don't kiss me, okay?"

It didn't make a lick of sense, but her attitude got to me. I had to shackle the urge to kiss her again, if only to be contrary. I had enough sense to know that was a bad idea.

"Tell me why it's a problem," I countered, feeling stubborn.

This was madness, and I didn't really care.

She rolled her eyes and sighed, rather dramatically if you asked me.

"Because you're... you're *you*," she offered.

Her annoyance and silly explanation got me back on firm footing in my mind, right where I could tease her.

"Right. That's exactly why you should kiss me," I said with a slow smile, knowing it would needle her.

I might not know Maisie as intimately as I'd like, but I knew how to get under her skin.

Her arms fell open, and she planted her hands on her hips. "Oh. My. God. You are so cocky. I think it's time for you to go."

"Wow, that's the thanks I get for fixing your hot water heater," I countered.

Her shoulders sagged a little. "I didn't mean..."

I pushed my hip off the counter. "It's okay, Maisie. Just teasing. You make it too easy for me."

She rolled her eyes and sighed again, but she'd lost her fire for a beat. "Well, thank you for fixing my hot water. I didn't realize how much I loved hot water until I didn't have it. Hey, you don't happen to know any tricks to get the water pressure as amazing as it is at the station?"

My brain went straight to the recollection of her standing there with the water running over her and soap bubbles the only thing covering her. I'd never admit it aloud, but that very recollection was what I'd jacked off to last night in the shower.

She was asking about water pressure, and I was wondering the fastest way to get her naked again.

Chapter Five

MAISIE

Don't think about list

1. Don't think about Beck
2. Don't think about how good it felt to kiss Beck
3. Don't think about how amazing his body felt against me
4. Don't think about how it seemed like he wanted me
5. Don't think about his hard cock
6. Don't think about the way he cupped my breast and made my nipples so tight they hurt

Oh hell. Listing about all the things I wasn't supposed to think about wasn't helping. At all. I could feel the slick heat between my thighs, and my nipples were tight and aching all over again. I was upstairs in my bedroom —the one and only bedroom I'd ever had that I really loved. The furnishings left behind by Gram had simple, clean lines. The queen size bed was built into the wall and low to the floor. Built in bookshelves ran along either side. All of the furniture was modern and wooden, finished in light colors. A skylight was directly above the bed. Even now, going on eleven at night, the silvery light of dusk fell through it. I could see the stars winking in the wispy sky.

My bedroom had its own personal bathroom with a shower and a soaking tub, which I'd come to adore. I recalled visiting this home before Gram had it updated. It had been warm and homey before, but the furnishings had been darker. Now everything was light and bright. I leaned back against the headboard and stared into the sky, willing thoughts of Beck out of my mind.

I loved writing lists. The habit started when I was little. I was the one who wrote the grocery lists for me and my dad. It was the only way I knew he'd remember to get what we needed. I'd gone from writing grocery lists as a little girl to writing lists for just about everything. Lists had gotten me through college and into my own apartment with barely two pennies to rub together. They were an organizational tool for me and kind of a mantra.

If I followed the lists, I'd get where I wanted to go. Right now, I desperately wanted to forget about Beck and that crazy, hot kiss. The best kiss I'd ever had actually.

I was restless and needy. I couldn't help but roll one of my nipples between my thumb and forefinger. My head fell against the wall with a thump. God, it wasn't even close to how it felt when Beck touched me, but I was so out of my mind horny and had been every since he left this afternoon. My thin tank top wasn't much of a barrier. I shifted my legs restlessly, the motion rubbing my wet pussy back and forth.

My phone buzzed on the shelf beside the bed. I rolled my head to see the screen lit up with a text. Still rolling my nipple lightly between my fingers, I snagged my phone with my free hand.

Hey Maze.

It was Beck. It's not as if he texted me often. In fact, any text from him was usually something to do with work. Oh hell. Just seeing his name on the screen made my channel clench. I wasn't wearing anything other than a tank top and a pair of men's boxers. That's what I preferred to sleep in. I could feel the wetness soaking into the thin cotton between my thighs. Only Beck had ever called me Maze. I secretly loved it because no one else called me that. I'd never mattered enough to anyone to have a nickname.

Here's the thing. I'll be kissing you again.

My finger hovered over the touch screen. I itched to reply, but none of it made sense. Why did he want me now? There was no doubt what I wanted. *Him*. Yet, I knew I wasn't the type of woman he usually went for. I also knew exactly what it would be if I let it go anywhere. Beck practically made flirting and casual dating a profession. Willow Brook was a small town, small enough that rumors traveled even when you didn't know anyone. By the time I'd been working at Fire & Rescue for a few weeks, I was well acquainted with the jokes about Beck. His nickname was Fun Time Fireman. For real.

I didn't doubt I'd have a good time with him, but I was pretty sure that would be a bad idea in the long run. I wouldn't say I was looking for more because I wasn't. Even if I felt a little lonely sometimes, I was quite content to mind my own business and be alone. I'd spent all of my life bouncing from one place to another. Living here in Gram's old house in Willow Brook for two whole years was a record for me. I was so relieved to have a place to call my own, I wasn't hoping for more. That would be tempting fate and asking for trouble, or so I figured.

So Beck and kissing and anything more were definitely heading into the danger zone. I didn't want to face what it might be like to try to work with him if we let things go any further. It would be awkward, and I'd be mortified if any of the guys found out. I stared at my phone screen, pondering whether to reply.

Bad idea.

I set my phone down and leaned my head back with another sigh. God, that was hard. It would feel so good to give into the madness of another kiss and a hell of lot more with Beck. But it was plain crazy, and I knew it.

My phone buzzed. Unable to resist, I snatched it off the shelf again.

Who knew you were so uptight? It was just a kiss. You know you want more. I definitely do.

Smoke practically came out of my ears. He had no idea that my life had been anything but boring before I landed in Willow Brook. Between being witness to my dad's rotating door on his bedroom, I was anything but uptight. I wasn't exactly crazy when I was in high school, but I'd had a few boyfriends, including my own personal rock-star-wannabe. I'd tried to be wild, but I'd actually found it a little boring, probably a side effect of being witness to my dad's constant quest for excitement that only left him looking like an irresponsible idiot.

I glared at my phone, my fingers itching to rapid fire some smartass reply. Beck had this way of getting to me, which had me half-wound up every time I encountered him. I took a few deep breaths, willing myself not to get too annoyed. Even worse, being annoyed with Beck fed straight into my desire for him. It was like a direct line into the liquid need sliding through my veins and making me hot all over.

Another deep breath.

I am NOT uptight. I know you're trying to annoy me, so just stop. It won't work.

His reply was swift.

Not trying to annoy you. Trying to turn you on. ;)

My belly flipped and his teasing comment had precisely the effect he wanted. Thank God he wasn't here to see it.

I turned my phone off and practically threw it on the shelf. I would *not* deign to respond further. That's what he was after.

I stared up through the skylight, trying to mentally chant my list of things not to think about, all of which centered around Beck. Instead, I remembered the feel of his lips against mine, his hard body—every inch of it—pressed against me, and the electricity sizzling in my veins when he touched me.

I didn't even realize I'd let out a soft moan until I heard it. My nipples were still tight, and the ache between my thighs wasn't going anywhere. Oh hell. There was only one way to get to sleep at this rate. With one hand cupping my breast and toying with my nipple, I slid the other down between my thighs. I was soaking wet, my folds slippery. I might never be stupid enough to let myself give in to Beck, but just thinking about him made me so hot, it didn't take much to bring me right to the edge. My channel clenched around my fingers, the hum of need I'd been fighting all day finally abating slightly.

Chapter Six

BECK

Smoke billowed around me, the air thick with it. I glanced up in the nick of time. A beam above gave way, and I dodged to the side. Moving on instinct alone with smoke obscuring everything, I shoved through a door at the end of the hallway. The smoke was thinner in here, and I could see the elderly woman in the bed.

"Cade! She's in here!" I called out through the window to my side.

I briefly checked the woman's pulse and breathed a sigh of relief to find one. Without waiting, I bundled her thin body into my arms and headed back down the hall blindly. Even though I couldn't see a damn thing, I was hot as hell inside my gear, and I'd entered this home close to when it was too late to be called safe, I was calm. As long as I was doing something, I could stay calm in the midst of chaos. The hallway felt long and I still had to make it down the stairs. I cornered the stair landing and moved swiftly down the last few, breaking into a jog once I hit the first floor. I could feel the fire quickening and the building close to turning into nothing but fuel.

I'd been a firefighter for over a decade now, so I was well familiar with the way a fire felt when it was taking over a structure. I could give you a scientific breakdown on the tipping point of a fire, but when I was in it, it was all about how it felt. I dashed through the doorway to the side of the house seconds before the ceiling above it collapsed. I kept moving, aiming straight for the ambulance waiting off to the side.

Once I got there, I paused and glanced down. The woman I'd carted out had wide blue eyes. She was looking right at me with a grin. What the hell?

Out of reflex, I smiled back.

"How ya doin'?" I asked.

"I think I'm fine," she said slowly, still grinning.

"What's that smile for?" I asked, pushing my respirator out of the way.

"Oh I've never been saved. It was rather exciting," she said with a little laugh. Her voice was raspy.

I returned her smile, relief rolling through me. No matter what, she appeared okay and that's all I needed to know.

"You looked asleep when I found you," I replied.

"Oh, I was. I didn't even have time to get scared. I woke up, and you were running down the hall with me. I have a story now," she said before she began coughing heavily.

Concern came on the heels of my relief. She was okay in the basic sense, but she probably needed oxygen as soon as possible.

"Hey, how are we doing?" Dana Halloran asked as she materialized magically by my side.

Dana was one of the EMT's. I was damn relieved because chipper as the woman in my arms was, she was elderly and from what I knew had likely been napping and inhaling smoke.

"Hey Dana, our friend here thinks it was fun to be saved, but I'm a little worried about her breathing," I explained, glancing from Dana to the woman.

"I didn't have a chance to get your name," I said when the woman looked up at me again on the heels of another coughing bout. "I'm Beck Steele."

Damn if this woman didn't miss a beat. She grinned again. "Oh my. Beck Steele sounds like a name straight out of an action movie."

A loud laugh came from behind me. I glanced back to see Cade Masters walking up to us. Cade was another superintendent who worked at Willow Brook Fire & Rescue with me. He'd just returned to town after almost three weeks out in the backcountry handling one of the massive wildfires plaguing Alaska's vast swathes of land.

He flashed a grin at me. "Beck Steele, action hero."

I rolled my eyes. "Same could be said for you."

"Yeah, but your name's more action hero," he countered with a wink.

Dana chuckled and addressed the woman. "I'm Dana, and I'd like to get you situated over there," she said, pointing to a wheeled bed by the ambulance. "I think a few minutes with oxygen might help you out."

The woman started coughing again. I could feel her frail body vibrating with each cough. I didn't wait to see what she might think and walked over to the bed, easing her onto it. Dana moved quickly and was wheeling over an oxygen tank inside of a few seconds. I helped prop her up on the pillows and tugged my helmet off, hooking the strap over my elbow.

Dana glanced to me as she adjusted the oxygen mask on the woman's face. "You made it out in the nick of time," she murmured.

I nodded. Now that we were clear, I spun around to look at the house. Cade had walked over and turned with me. The home was falling into itself now. We'd gotten a call too late to do much other than rescue this afternoon. It was high season for fires in Alaska, and we'd had a long, dry summer so far. The home we'd been called to was on the outskirts of town and adjacent to a large swath of spruce forest. For reasons we'd yet to sort out, a fire had broken out in the trees beside the home. A low hanging branch was too close to the house and the fire spread. Aside from two teen boys and this grandmother, no one else had been home. The fire had been in full swing by the time the call came in from a neighbor who spotted the flames from over a mile away.

Alaska was a great place to live if you

wanted privacy. The downside to privacy was areas where homes were spread so far apart, no one was nearby to notice a fire early on. I watched while the crew positioned hoses and worked on controlling the burn.

I glanced to Cade and then back to Dana. "It was close, but we made it." I looked to the woman who appeared to be breathing more steadily now.

She tugged at her oxygen mask.

Dana eased it away. "Need something?" Dana asked.

"I'm fine now. That thing is annoying," the woman declared.

I couldn't help but laugh. "Mind telling us your name?"

"Susie. Susie Smith, the most boring name ever," she announced. "Oh and before you go wondering how that fire started, I'll tell you."

Dana arched a brow and glanced my way. I shrugged.

"The police chief will want to talk with you, but go ahead and fill us in."

"It's that idiot who lives down the road and drives his loud ass truck all the time. I swear, he confuses his truck with his penis," she announced with a roll of her eyes and another bout of coughing.

Dana promptly put the oxygen mask back on Susie. I assured her I'd send the police chief over to talk with her. There was no shortage of idiots who drove trucks around Willow Brook, so I didn't really know who Susie meant.

Dana and another EMT got busy rolling Susie's bed up to the ambulance. I looked back to Cade. "Well, I'll call this one a win. Everyone got out safe and sound."

Cade shrugged. "With ya there. I called back to the station. They're rounding up the new guys in training to bring 'em out here. This will need to be monitored until it's out. Damn shame. This house wasn't that old."

"Any idea how it started?"

"Not yet. Best guess is sparks blew over from a fire down the road. I'm gonna guess the fire in question was started by the guy who confuses his truck with his penis," Cade replied with a roll of his eyes. He knocked his fire helmet against the tire of the truck we stood beside. "Ride back with me?" he asked.

At my nod, we turned in unison. I stopped to check in with Thad Mason who was one of the foremen on my crew. Leaving him in charge, I departed with Cade who had been born and raised in Willow Brook with me. I'd known him forever, yet he'd moved away for a chunk of time and had only been back for a little while. He'd come back the same old Cade—on the quiet side, but funny and solid as they came for a friend. He'd finally seen straight and married his high school sweetheart, Amelia, not too long ago. They'd had a classic misunderstanding break up years back, and Cade had stayed away from Willow Brook because of it.

It was damn good to have him back and finally happy again. Cade was a one-woman man through and through. I'd never quite seen the appeal because it wasn't my personality, but when it came to Amelia, Cade couldn't see past that woman. I figured it was a damn good thing she had it just as bad for him.

I leaned my head back as he drove the truck down the winding dirt road that led away from the burning house and back to the highway. I rolled my head sideways. His dark brown hair was a sweaty mess. I knew I looked just as bad and could feel the soot on my face.

"You wanna grab a few beers at Wildlands after we check in at the station?" I asked.

"Sure. Amelia will probably want to meet us. That okay?"

I chuckled. "It's always okay, man."

Cade glanced my way and flashed a grin. "Guess so. You wouldn't see me much if it wasn't."

"Nah. I sure wouldn't. I've given up on you ever getting past being whipped by her."

Cade shrugged. "Me too. It's all good though. Trust me, you'll find the right woman and you won't know what hit you."

I chuckled along with him and steered the conversation onto other matters. I'd never admit it, but the only woman who came to mind when Cade teased was Maisie.

Hell, I could hardly stop thinking about her since the other day. It had been a full week since I'd walked in on her naked in the showers at the station. Six days since I kissed her at her house. That totaled up to one hundred and sixty-eight hours that I'd barely been able to stop thinking about her. If I subtracted seven hours of sleep a night, that left me with just under one hundred and twenty waking hours for her to sashay about in my thoughts. The woman had fucking taken up residence in my brain.

I'd jacked off to the memory of the way she felt pressed up against me yet again last night when I couldn't sleep. She'd been nothing but appropriate around the station since then. She'd also never replied to my last text. I couldn't resist baiting her here and there, but that was nothing new. Except now it was more loaded, at least for me. I suppose it was fair to say my cock was loaded.

Thank fuck it had been a busy week around the station. We were handling a low level wildfire on the outskirts of Willow Brook and had responded to various and sundry emergencies almost daily. That was about the only thing that nudged my mind off of Maisie.

MAISIE

"Oh come on, Maisie. The only way you'll make more friends around here is to actually go somewhere to meet people," Susannah Gilmore said.

"I see plenty of people here," I countered.

Susannah rested her chin in her hand and glared at me. "I thought I was stubborn. Then I met you."

A laugh bubbled up as I looked across the counter at her. "You *are* really stubborn."

Susannah rolled her eyes and sighed. "Come out for dinner with me. It won't kill you, and you might even have fun," she cajoled.

"Fine. I'll come."

I didn't really have a reason not to go,

other than I tended to be a 'to myself' kind of person by default. Susannah was the only other woman who worked with me. She was a badass hotshot firefighter and could hold her own with all of the guys. She'd intimidated the hell out of me at first, but I'd slowly gotten to know her. She was funny and smart and nice. She also happened to be cute as hell. She was medium height with strawberry blonde hair and bright blue eyes. Being a firefighter meant she was insanely fit, although she still had curves. She'd just returned with her crew from a three-week stint out on a fire in the middle of Alaska and had decided my company was required to celebrate her return. I figured it couldn't hurt to try to be social.

Not much later, I walked beside Susannah into Wildlands Lodge & Bar. Wildlands was one of many wilderness lodges scattered about Alaska. The lodge consisted of a sprawling timber frame hotel, which had been expanded and modernized. The place was booked to capacity all summer long. It was situated beside Swan Lake, the center-piece of Willow Brook. Between Willow Brook's location within a short drive from Anchorage, the view of Denali in the distance, and Swan Lake, hordes of tourists passed through town every summer.

When we stepped inside, I glanced around, taking in the crowded restaurant. I hadn't been here much. I'd started to feel like Willow Brook was truly my home, but that didn't mean I was a social butterfly. Willow Brook was a popular destination in southcentral Alaska due to its location, but it also served as a hub for planes that arrayed out across the Alaskan geography, taking tourists all over the state for wilderness trips. As I scanned the faces in the room, I saw a few familiar ones, but not many.

Susannah hooked her arm through mine and dragged me through the tables. She'd been insistent lately that I needed to start making more friends. Though Susannah had bossed me into coming here tonight, I hadn't clued her in to my worry that I might run into Beck. This was definitely his stomping ground. I shoved him out of my mind, knowing any effort to kick him out of my thoughts would only be temporary. Clusters of tables were scattered throughout the large restaurant with a bar running along one side. As we walked through, a female voice called Susannah's name. She immediately redirected our path, walking me over to a table where

Amelia Masters and Lucy Caldwell were seated.

"Hey there," Susannah said. "Please tell me you were saving this table for us."

Amelia grinned and took a long draw off her beer. "Of course."

Susannah sat down across from Amelia, and I slipped into a chair beside her. They were seated at a large round table in the corner. I figured they were expecting more company, otherwise there'd be no point in snagging such a large table. With the crowd here, they'd be fending off people if the table weren't filled soon.

"How's it going, Maisie?" Amelia asked. "It's good to see you out and about."

I busied my hands, snagging a menu from the center of the table and starting to flip through it. "Oh, it's good. How are you? Haven't seen you at the station lately."

Lucy elbowed Amelia in the side. "That's because she's working too hard. I'm a workaholic and even I think it's too much."

A waitress paused by our table and took drink orders. Conversation carried on around me as Susannah commiserated with the grueling summer work schedules in Alaska. I knew Amelia in passing. She was married to Cade Masters, another hotshot superintendent at Willow Brook Fire & Rescue. Apparently, they'd been high school sweethearts years ago, and things had ended ugly over a misunderstanding. I wasn't hip to all the gossip around Willow Brook, but their reunion had half the town swooning, so it had been hard to miss.

I happened to think Cade was a great guy. He was much easier for me to deal with than Beck, mostly because I didn't get all flustered around him. Amelia often stopped by the station to see him. To be honest, she was slightly intimidating. She ran her own construction company, named, of all things, Kick A** construction. I figured she could probably kick my ass, but I liked her. Funny and nice, she was easily as tall as most men and beautiful with amber hair and eyes. I knew Lucy, but not quite as well. I saw Lucy maybe once in a blue moon at the station if she stopped by with Amelia. Lucy worked with Amelia. She was a startling contrast to Amelia. At a glance, you'd think she was girly. With her fair hair, blue eyes, and petite, curvy build, she was drop dead gorgeous. As far as I could tell, the last thing she thought about was her looks. She typically looked as if she'd just stepped off of a construction job site.

Once the waitress returned with our drinks, my ears perked up at Amelia's comment. "Cade'll be here in a bit. Did you come straight from the station?"

Susanna nodded as she snagged a menu from the center of the table. "Yeah, but the guys weren't back from their last run. I told Maisie it was time for her to go somewhere other than home after work."

Lucy caught my eyes. "Isn't it fun to be bossed around by our friends?" she asked with a wry grin.

The warm empathy in her gaze helped me relax a little. "I suppose being bossed isn't the worst thing," I offered with a small laugh. "I don't get out much. I'm happy to just work and go home, but Susannah seems to think I need more friends."

"Oh I get it. I like to keep to myself, but some people around here think that's a sacrilege," Lucy said, sending a pointed glance Amelia's way.

Amelia rolled her eyes. "Oh cut it out. You have friends, and you're the one who gave me a hard time after I got too busy with Cade."

Lucy rolled her eyes even harder. "Yeah, well that's because you were so gaga over him, no one ever saw you."

Susanna chuckled. "My friends keep me sane. I spend too much time with guys anyway, so I need nights like this."

Amelia and Lucy chatted about some job they were working on. Susannah gave the update on the wildfire she'd just returned from after a three-week stint with her crew. Susannah was on a different crew than both Cade and Beck.

Amelia was nodding along. "Any chance you're gonna tell me they've got that fire under control?"

Susannah shook her head. "Not yet. We made good progress containing the fire, but there's plenty more to do. You worrying about Cade's crew rotating out there?"

Amelia shrugged. "Define worry. It's his job, so I have to live with it. He said his crew will probably head out in another week or two if it's not fully contained."

Sometimes I wondered what it was like to be close to a hotshot firefighter. I'd become friendly with all of them. I worried about them when they were out in the field, but I imagined it was a different kind of worry for Amelia.

"I bet it's hard when he's away like that," I commented.

Amelia twisted her mouth slightly. "Always," she said softly. "Not much I can do about it though. It's what he does and he loves it."

Lucy piped up. "I always tell her, statistically speaking he's more likely to get in a car accident than he is to get hurt out fighting a fire. I know it's cold comfort, but I have to say something."

Amelia grinned. "And I love you for it."

"I bet it's hard. I've pretty much given up on finding someone. Most men are not gonna want to deal with the risk my job entails. Unless I end up married to a firefighter," Susannah said with a rueful grin.

"Who's to say you won't marry a firefighter? You've got about fifty to choose from among the crews here," Lucy said with a sly smile.

Susannah rolled her eyes at that. "Right, like I'm gonna go for one of the guys that I work with. I can't even imagine."

"I might joke, but I get it. Hell, I'm an electrician and a construction worker. I'm probably not gonna do the guy thing, and that's good with me. Cheers to our independence," Lucy said, lifting her drink aloft in a faux toast.

Amelia laughed and glanced to me. "Don't tell me you're gonna say the same thing too?"

"Probably. My life is just fine how it is. I've got a good job, a good house and a peaceful life. I don't mind keeping it that way."

Amelia looked slightly dismayed as she glanced among us. "You know, relationships aren't horrible."

Lucy looked from her to Susannah and me. "This is her new thing. She thinks I'm missing out," Lucy said drolly. "I keep reminding her not everyone gets a second chance with the love of their life."

"Have you even given anyone a chance?" Amelia asked with a roll of her eyes. She started to say something else, but was interrupted when someone called her name.

I glanced over to see Cade approaching. Beck was a few steps behind him, pausing to talk to someone at the bar. Cade was a classic, rugged Alaskan firefighter. He had rumpled brown curls, green eyes, and a body to die for. I'd gotten used to the fact that any man who was a hotshot firefighter had a body practically carved from stone. Their work was grueling and so physically demanding, it blew me away. In short though, I was surrounded by men who could fill a calendar with hotness. I didn't feel a damn thing for any of them. Except Beck.

Cade reached our table, hooked his hand over a chair nearby and slid it up right beside Amelia. He dropped a kiss on the side of her neck as he did. The intimacy between them was so obvious, it was almost a physical manifestation. I wondered what it was like to have something like that. It wasn't something I really thought much about. There was only one person I could count on—me. At least, that's what I told myself when I occasionally considered that it might be nice to have something like what Amelia and Cade shared.

Beck started approaching us again after he finished chatting with someone at the bar. I willed my eyes not to wander in his direction, but my eyes were stronger than my will. He walked with an unconscious swagger, his muscled arms swinging with ease. Dear God. His arms. Even his arms turned me on. My low belly clenched, and my pulse kicked up a notch.

Great. Just what I need. A night at the bar with Beck where I'm a mess inside. Why did I let Susannah talk me into this?

Maybe because you were hoping you'd see him.

Shut up.

As Beck threaded his way through the tables and the light crowd, a woman touched him on the shoulder and threw a flirtatious glance his way. He laughed at whatever she said, flashing one of his devastating grins. I wished, oh how I wished, I didn't fall for his grin the way I did. Every time he bestowed one upon me, I felt like a top spinning and lighting up inside. That feeling would invariably follow with a harsh reminder that Beck was practically a professional flirt.

Chapter Eight

BECK

I headed straight for the table where I could see Maisie sitting with a few friends. Conveniently, the only empty chair happened to be right beside her. I slid into it quickly. I looked around the table, greeting everyone individually before finally allowing myself to look at Maisie. Lust jolted me at the sight of her plump lips and those wide brown eyes.

"Hey Maisie, didn't expect to see you here. Come to think of it, I don't know if I've ever seen you here," I said.

Her eye roll was quick. It usually was around me. I fucking loved it because it meant I was getting to her.

"It's not usually my speed," she said, her tone snippy.

"What's wrong with dinner with friends?"

I could feel her annoyance notch a little higher. Honestly, she was like a cactus around me. Much as I enjoyed needling her in small ways, it fed into the desire I could barely keep in check around her.

With my pulse running along on high idle and my cock so hard I had to shift in my seat, I bit back the urge to keep teasing her.

Susannah's gaze bounced from me to Maisie. "Exactly what I told her. Dinner with friends is not a bad thing. Maisie's more central to the station than all of us, and she hardly ever hangs out with us," she said with a grin.

Maisie rolled her eyes at Susannah. "Well, I'm here now."

The waitress stopped by our table. Drinks and food were ordered, and conversation carried on. Much as I wanted to relax, I was finding it slightly distracting and challenging to have the ridiculously tempting Maisie sitting right beside me.

Cade was in the middle of regaling the rest of the table with an amusing story about a moose encounter the last time his crew had been out in the backcountry. I glanced to Maisie, giving in to the urge to touch her with a little nudge of my elbow. Immediately, she looked up, her cheeks pinkening. My cock responded accordingly.

"So how've you been?" I asked conversationally, snagging a sweet potato fry and popping it in my mouth.

Because my eyes were willful, they kept flicking down to her breasts. Her navy t-shirt pulled tight across them. My mind flashed to the feel of her taut nipple and the delicious weight of her breast cupped in my palm.

I took a gulp of my beer.

"Fine," she said with a small shrug.

I took another drag on my beer and pondered my situation. It shouldn't be difficult to have a casual conversation with her, but I was bound tight with need.

I was relieved when she continued.

"Everything go okay on the call? I saw the report that everybody was out safe. Do you know what caused the fire?" she asked.

"Best guess is some embers blew over from a fire down the road, but we don't know for sure yet. It's too bad the call came in late. By the time we got there, there wasn't much to do other than make sure everybody was out safe. There were two teenage kids and their grandmother in the house."

"Oh, is everyone okay?"

"Yup. A little smoke inhalation for the

grandmother. They took her to the hospital to get checked out, but she should be fine. The house is a total loss, but I call it a win as long as nobody gets hurt."

She nodded and took a swallow of her drink. My eyes lingered on her throat as she leaned back. I was so tempted to lean over and drag my tongue along the sensitive skin there. I wasn't accustomed to having need rule me the way it did with Maisie. It was impossible for me to forget how she'd looked naked and wet in the shower and then how she felt when I kissed her.

"Thanks again for fixing my hot water heater. It's great to have hot water."

"Of course. Anytime you need help with something like that, just let me know," I said, managing to draw my words out and wink. I couldn't help my reflexive response. Fucking perfect.

Her cheeks flushed deeper, and she looked down at her burger and took a giant bite. Even that was sexy.

I was still mystified she hadn't asked for help in the first place. "Do me a favor and don't make yourself wait next time," I added.

"I probably should've said something sooner, but I'm not used to having a whole bunch of guys around that would help me with things like that."

"Well, you definitely have me," I said.

I hadn't meant to flirt, but it was a fall-back habit for me. Just now, I didn't mind.

Not when I saw her pulse flutter in her neck and her eyes narrow as she looked up.

"No need to look like that. You've got plenty of girls here to flirt with. Why don't you go find one?"

I doubted she meant it, but her words stung a little. "Hey, I'm here just to hang out with some friends."

She eyed me for a beat and took another gulp from her drink. "I may not spend much time around here, but I know what the rumors are. This is right up your alley. Plenty of girls to pick up, most of them just passing through, so you can love em' and leave em.' Don't look at me like one of them," she snapped.

I liked to have fun and made no bones about it, but I didn't appreciate how she pegged me for some jerk. Uncertain how to reply, I stared at her for a moment.

I finally lifted a shoulder in a shrug and took a swig of my beer. "Whatever, Maisie. I won't pretend to be something I'm not, but I'm not an asshole. I like to have fun, and I like to tease. It is what it is. Tonight, I'm just here for dinner with my friends."

"Don't give Beck too hard of a time. All he ever does is flirt. He's pretty harmless," Lucy interjected with a roll of her eyes and a soft grin tossed my way.

If possible, Lucy was more gun shy than Maisie when it came to men. I hadn't known her to date anyone since high school. She was a good friend though. I smiled across the table at her, gratified at least she didn't think I was an ass.

"See, even Lucy says I'm not that bad."

Lucy started laughing, and Amelia joined in.

"Lucy went to high school with us too, so we know he's harmless. He's always there if you need him. He's a professional flirt, but that's about it," Amelia added.

I shook my head lightly and glanced to Cade. "What do I gotta do to get these girls off my back? Shack up like you?"

Cade merely laughed and hooked his arm over Amelia's shoulder. "That would certainly do it."

"Well, you might be harmless, but I can't imagine you settling down," Lucy said with a low laugh.

Maisie stayed quiet, and my gut clenched

a little. I wasn't looking for love and never had been. I didn't quite know what to make of the flaming hot chemistry between us, but I was pretty sure it would be best for both of us if we let it end with that one wild and crazy kiss. It had been a big enough mistake as it was. Yet, somehow I didn't want to. I wanted more and hell if I knew what to make of that.

Chapter Nine

MAISIE

Eventually the party started to break up. I said my goodbyes and went to the restroom. I washed my hands and splashed water on my cheeks. I was still flushed. It made me feel ridiculous the way I was around Beck. I stared at myself in the mirror and wondered what he saw in me. My dark, crazy curls stuck out willy-nilly even though I'd pulled them back in a ponytail this morning. One errant curl hung loose on my cheek. My eyes were a little big and dark in my face, or so I thought. I looked at myself with a critical eye. I didn't think much about how I looked. It wasn't something I'd ever had much time to contemplate. Makeup wasn't my thing either. I saw wide brown eyes, dark lashes, and round cheeks. I'd always been a little bit round all over. Though they were in the right places, my curves were definitely enthusiastic. I patted my face dry and headed out the back door of Wildlands to the parking lot, telling myself I'd get past my body's willful response to Beck.

———

A few days later, I proved myself even more social by grabbing a late coffee at Firehouse Café after work with Susannah and Lucy. I climbed in my truck afterwards, only to realize I didn't have my purse. A quick trip back inside, and it was nowhere to be found. I tugged my phone out of my pocket and quickly texted Susannah to ask if she'd seen it before she left.

She replied in a flash.

Nope. Didn't see one. Maybe you left it at the station?

Probably. Thanks.

That's twice you survived a social event. Now you won't get away with telling me no all the time. :)

Don't get crazy.

At that, I hurried back out to the parking

lot, climbed in my truck and headed for the station.

Within a few minutes, I was walking into the station. All year long, we had back up emergency call support from the Anchorage Fire Department. Unless I was on duty, the calls routed through there. Our crews were also set up to receive calls from home. Unlike the old-school fire stations where they actually had people sleeping there, our station didn't. It was dark and quiet. I headed into the back and found my purse right where I'd left it in my locker. I walked back out front, pausing at the counter. It might be odd, but I found the station comforting. I'd been at this job longer than any I'd had before. I loved it too. I didn't get paid a ton, but I had enough to cover all of my bills and start saving a little. I'd been stubborn about my hot water heater because I didn't want to put a dent in my savings. For the first time in my life, I had more than five hundred dollars saved up. The only time I had savings before, I'd used all of it to fly up here before Gram passed away.

This place felt sort of like a home for me. The whole front counter was mine. Nobody else really went back there. We had a few alternates to cover in emergencies but that was it. It made me feel responsible, and I loved that feeling. Out of habit, I quickly powered up my computer and scanned the list of calls that had come in recently. Tonight had been pretty quiet so far. A few short calls were logged, including a truck engine fire on the outskirts of town. I turned my computer off again and double-checked the front doors even though I hadn't even come in through the front. I headed into the back again. Just as I entered the hallway, I heard footsteps.

There would be no reason for anybody to be here unless a call had come in and I'd just checked. The lights were off since I hadn't bothered to turn them on when I came in. The only light available was from a small light that remained on over the sink in the kitchen area. It cast a soft, silvery glow in the room. The footsteps rounded the corner from the back door, and Beck stepped into view.

My pulse took off at a gallop, and my breath caught.

He walked toward me, hot as hell in his faded jeans and t-shirt. That was pretty much a uniform for him. His clothes hugged his body like a lover, every muscled inch out-lined. He didn't even have to try, and he was so sexy it was obscene. His arms swung easily with his slightly lazy swagger. I doubt he even tried to swagger. He just did, that's the kind of guy he was. All man. He stopped a few feet away from me and caught my eyes.

"I wondered whose truck that was," he said. "What are you doing here this late, Maisie?"

Heat coiled low in my belly, and my pulse lunged. Great, just great. I'd avoided being alone with him for a full week, and somehow I managed to run into him in the middle of the night, alone and only feet away from the showers where he'd seen me completely naked. I swallowed and willed my pulse to slow down. All I needed to do was act normal and then get out of this as fast as humanly possible.

"Oh, I forgot my purse," I said, holding it up as if he needed verification. "I'm off for the next two days, and I figured I'd need it."

Of course you need your purse. Obvious much?

My snide side was always quick on the take when Beck was around.

He was quiet, his dark green gaze shifting from knowing to teasing as his eyes held mine.

"Ah, you forgot your purse."

He nodded slowly, his simple response instantly annoying me.

"Yes. That's it. I forgot my purse."

I held it up again, giving it another little shake as if I needed to really prove it. His low laugh sent a shiver down my spine.

"I see that. I didn't think you were lying Maisie, that's not really your style."

I tried to take a deep breath, but air was hard to come by, especially when my heart was beating like crazy, and I was hot all over. Again.

Being alone with him wasn't comfortable. It reminded me precisely of the last time I was alone with him. He'd kissed me senseless. No matter how hard I tried to tell myself I didn't want him, I did. Badly.

I had to bite the inside of my cheek to stay quiet and wondered what to say to gracefully exit myself from this situation. He'd stopped a few feet away from the run of counters along the back wall. His eyes stayed locked to me. One hand was hooked in his pocket, and he rolled his shoulder absent-mindedly. He did that often enough—because dammit I paid attention to him—sometimes I wondered if he'd ever injured that shoulder.

"You never replied last weekend," he said abruptly, his voice low, taut and husky.

The sound of it alone sent another shiver down my spine. Damn, my body's reaction to him was ridiculous. I didn't want to want him, but I wanted him like crazy. When I stayed quiet, solely because I was paralyzed by the need flooding me, Beck arched a brow.

Without him saying a word, I knew he was teasing me for the fact that I couldn't even seem to reply. I straightened my shoulders and took in gulp of air before mustering a glare.

"My last reply was the only one you'll get on that topic."

He pulled his hand out of his pocket, his phone coming with it. Inside of a second, he was scanning his screen. "Ah, you said it was a bad idea."

He spun his phone idly in his hand, watching me, the air loaded and humming around us. It felt as if he were touching me, my skin prickling everywhere his eyes landed. Maybe ten feet separated us. I stood right in front of the showers. In a flash, he closed the distance between us, his stride long and sure. He stopped in front of me, too close for comfort.

"Why are you being so stubborn about this?" he asked, his voice gruff.

"About what?" I hedged.

I was determined not to take his bait. As

soon as I said that, I realized I had. He wasn't one to dodge topics, and he'd call me out for even trying to do that. A dark brow rose in a slash, his mouth curled up at one corner, and that knowing, teasing glint in his eyes was in full force.

"Can't even talk about it," he observed.

I had to bite the inside of my cheek—hard—to keep from swearing at him. Why, oh why did he get to me so easily?

"I'm not talking about it because there's nothing to talk about. We kissed. Once. It won't happen again. If you're looking for someone to pick up, I suggest you head back to the bar."

This only led to his grin widening. Oh hell. His grin was dangerous to me. Heat spun in circles in my belly, my nipples tightened, and I wished like hell I had actually bothered to put my jacket on because I knew he could see them pressing against my t-shirt. The only thing on my side was the dim lighting. He probably couldn't see the flush on my face and neck. I was hot and prickly all over. I swallowed, marshaling myself.

"I don't want anyone else. I want you, Maisie."

Oh. My. God. It was a miracle I didn't melt into a puddle at his feet. I'd only fantasized—against my will fantasies, mind you—about Beck for two years. The list I'd written of all the ways I wasn't supposed to think about him had turned out to be utterly useless. Trust me, having him be this blunt about wanting me made me a little bit crazy inside.

He continued, "I want you, you want me. I don't want to go back to the bar for anybody else, in fact."

He drew that last word out. How in the hell could the word *fact* sound sexy coming from his mouth? It was, trust me, it was. Oh God, I was so screwed. Correction: I wanted to be screwed. By Beck. *Now.*

He stepped closer, lifting one hand and trailing his finger down along the collar of my t-shirt. My pulse went from wild to wilder, racing so hard and fast, it took my breath away. My channel clenched in response to his touch. All he had to do was touch me with one finger, and I was mush inside and out. I felt ridiculous, almost melting in place as his finger followed down along my collar, pausing at the point of the V where it dipped down between my breasts.

I hoped like hell he couldn't actually feel my heart beating. With his fingertip resting just inches away from where it pounded away under my ribs, he was quiet. His eyes scanned my face, dipping down and then coming back up. The path of his eyes felt like a caress, sending hot shivers chasing through me.

"I'm not the guy you think I am, Maisie. You have no idea what I think."

I was discovering I had a serious weakness for his voice like this. I was fairly certain he could persuade me to do anything right now. Anything he said in that low, gruff, almost whisper was a straight shot to my body's desire for him. I forced myself to focus.

Thank God he didn't expect me to reply because I wasn't sure I could.

"Don't get me wrong," he continued. "I love to flirt, but when I have one woman on my mind, that's the *only* woman on my mind. Right now, that's *you*. Let's just see where things go because this feeling isn't going anywhere. You know it, and I know it."

I stared at him, willing myself to be sensible when I was feeling anything but. I wanted to do far more than simply fantasize about him. As far as I was concerned, sex was kind of fun, but nothing amazing. I considered that maybe if we actually did something about this, I'd realize the fantasy was better than reality. These heated thoughts would fade into nothing after that. I could stop thinking like a crazy woman. I didn't dare share my train of thought. I stayed quiet, looking at him, and then next thing I knew, my thoughts were tumbling out.

"Here's the deal. We get it out of our systems and then you keep your mouth shut. Forever," I said flatly.

My voice sounded normal, but it belied the tornado of emotion swirling inside of me. Desire, need, and the wild thrum of giving into it pounded through my body.

"Of course," he said, cocking his head to the side and looking surprised.

I wasn't sure if he was surprised that I was actually willing to go along with this, or surprised that I asked him to keep it quiet. I felt the need to clarify because it was really important to me that no one viewed me as one of Beck's flings.

"We work together, Beck. Maybe it's nothing to you. But the way the guys might look at me if they think I'm just another one of your flings, well..."

My words trailed off because his gaze had sobered. I wasn't sure what I saw in his eyes, but I wondered if it was hurt. Not much, just a little. I fumbled ahead. "I mean, your reputation precedes you. You're 'Fun time fireman,' or whatever."

A low chuckle escaped from him. "Okay, fair enough. I'm not the one that brags about people that I'm with, but I joke around a lot. I can see why you might get that idea."

"Don't go thinking I'm saying I want something serious. It's just I work here, and I don't want the other guys to think..." I flushed because I didn't know how else to explain what I meant. "It's just this can't go anywhere," I finally said.

Beck stared at me, the air around us getting heavy, and then nodded sharply. His teasing gaze had faded away. The air went from weighted to electric inside of a second.

Chapter Ten

BECK

Maisie stood in front of me, her curls tumbling around her shoulders. I didn't think I'd ever seen her with her hair down before. It was a sight to behold—pure glory. Her curls alone were sinful, so wild and unruly. She always had them in a ponytail or shoved under a baseball cap. Her wide eyes held mine. I was close enough to see the flutter of her pulse in her neck. It was a relief to know she felt something, though I doubted she was as caught up in desire as I was. I'd been out of my fucking mind over it ever since I'd kissed her last week.

Running into her at dinner the other night had only made matters worse. Maisie was showing me the limits to my control, an entirely unfamiliar feeling for me. There were so many women passing through town all summer long that it was easy to enjoy casual, guaranteed-to-end relationships. I didn't think much of it. Yet Maisie didn't make anything easy. Even though I could sense the desire coming off of her in waves, she was close to glaring at me. Damn. I loved to ruffle her. The only downside was whenever she was annoyed with me, it turned up the dial on my desire.

She'd practically stunned me into silence just now. I'd been prepared to argue with her, yet she just said we could do this. The unspoken *this* being to take that kiss much further. My cock had been hard since the second I looked across the room and saw her. It was just us here now. The station was deserted and dark with nothing more than the soft glow of a single light in this room. My mind flashed to the sight of Maisie in the showers. Oh hell. She was so fucking gorgeous, and she had no idea the effect she had on me.

My fingertip rested at the V in her shirt. I could easily, so easily, slide my hand down to cup one of her breasts. But if she wasn't going to argue the point, I was going to take this slow and wring every ounce of need out of us. I caught the end of one of her curls and wound it around my finger. Her breath hitched, and my cock throbbed. In a distant corner of my mind, I wondered if this was a good idea. I brushed that worry aside. Two long years of lust running on high idle in my body whenever I was anywhere near Maisie, and my engine had been revved to madness since that kiss.

I gave her curl a slow tug and let it go. It bounced against her cheek. Her breath drew in sharply, and her eyes narrowed when I chuckled. Little did she know how her getting annoyed with me only served to amp up the lust burning through me. Hell if I knew why, but Maisie was the one and only woman who had that effect on me. I loved teasing her if only because it was so much damn fun.

"Really, Beck? You're pulling my hair? Isn't that a bit childish?"

Lust jolted me when she rested a hand on her hip and rolled her eyes. Oh, she had no idea what she'd just done.

I kept a leash on my need, just barely, and arched a brow. "I suppose that depends. I can think of reasons to pull your hair that have absolutely nothing to do with being childish," I drawled.

It took most of my willpower to keep from twining her hair around my hand and yanking her to me. The one and only reason I held back was to see how she responded.

Her breath drew in sharply, and her eyes darkened. The backs of my fingers rested just below her collarbone. I could feel her heartbeat kick up its pace.

"So, let's make things clear," I said, my voice coming out rough.

I didn't feel in control, hardly at all. But she'd just told me we'd get this—whatever she meant *this* to be—out of our systems. She'd also demanded I forever keep it quiet. I didn't mind that. I understood why she wouldn't want the other guys to know anything. I couldn't tell her the plain truth—I'd go flat crazy if I thought any of the guys I worked with were interested in her in any way. Hell, that fateful afternoon I'd walked in on her in the showers I'd done some fast talking to keep the guys from finding her there. I didn't want anyone to know how fucking gorgeous she was.

Her gorgeous brown eyes—like dark chocolate—held mine. Inches away from her, I was close enough to see her thick lashes curled against her cheeks. I wasn't used to noticing things like this. Hell, I even thought her freckles were hot. They were scattered across her nose and cheeks, and I wanted to follow them where they led me.

"What do you mean?" she asked, her voice husky.

"Well, you said we'd get this out of our systems. What do you mean by *this*?"

Her cheeks flushed a deeper shade of pink. I couldn't see too well in the dim light, but I was close enough not to miss it. Hot damn. Maisie hot and bothered was a turn on beyond my wildest fantasies. I could feel my cock straining against my zipper. I'd jacked off more times than I wanted to admit to the memory of kissing her and the sight of her naked in the showers.

She bit her lip. Oh hell. I was trying to be sort of a gentleman here, and she had to go and do that. Her pearly white teeth dented her plump bottom lip. She rolled the corner of it and twisted her mouth slightly before sighing.

"Um, this," she said, dropping her hand from her hip and gesturing between us.

I eyed her, thinking I could just say fuck it and fuck her right now. If this were any woman other than Maisie, that's what I'd be doing. But this was Maisie, and she made me feel all kinds of things. I might want her like crazy, but I wasn't about to take things further than she intended.

I couldn't help but slide my hand up to trace along her collarbone. She was so close, and I needed to touch her. "Right. To me, *this* would be whatever we started last week. *This* would be not stopping until I'm buried inside of you and you're screaming for more. Is that what you mean by *this*?"

Her lips parted, and her pulse raced under the translucent skin of her neck. I couldn't help but dip my head and drag my tongue over it. She was salty and sweet, and I almost groaned. At nothing more than the subtle taste of her.

I forced myself to lift my head. Her eyes were dark, and her breath came in sharp little pants.

"Well?" I asked.

"Yes..." she whispered on a breath.

Thank fuck. I was at the end of my rope. I threaded my hand in her hair and finally—fucking finally—fit my mouth over hers again. Kissing her was like a drug. She didn't hold back, not even a little. I tugged her to me, one hand tangled in her hair and the other sliding down her back in a heated pass to cup her bottom. Did I mention how perfect her body was? She was all dips and swells, every curve lush and soft. My fingers sank into the give of her ass, and I growled into her mouth. God, I'd been thinking about the feel of her for too long. Having it real was a hot jolt of relief and madness at once.

We'd come together in front of a long run of counters against the back wall and the showers just beyond. I had plenty of ideas about those showers, but right now, I spun us toward the counter. In a few fumbling strides, her hips bumped against it. I slid both hands down to cup her hips and lift her onto the counter, pulling her tight against me. Oh yes. I could feel the damp heat between her thighs against my cock.

I didn't ponder much when it came to sex. I was a man of action. Just like firefighting, I worked on instinct, but I was in control. Always. Just now with Maisie, I was learning there were some things I'd never experienced. Namely, being out of control. I was usually measured and orchestrated with what I did. Not with her.

Our kiss was a hot, wild, wet mess. I couldn't get close enough. I devoured her mouth. Our tongues tangled, while my hands roamed her body. Just as I remembered with vivid clarity from our kiss, she was all soft curves. It was a pure high to have her pressed up against me. I needed to taste more of her and dragged my lips from hers, trailing a wet path down her neck. Her skin pebbled everywhere my lips landed. She made these hot, breathy sounds—something between a breath and a moan—that drove me fucking wild.

Between that and her hips rocking against me, I was barely, just barely, hanging onto a thread of control. I licked along the collar of her shirt, right down between her breasts. Impatient, I shoved her t-shirt up, leaning back just enough to yank it up over her head. She was quite helpful when it got caught on her wild hair.

"Dammit," she murmured and deftly reached up, untangling a few curls caught in the collar before tossing the shirt to the floor.

Her eyes snagged mine—liquid brown and pooled with need. I'd never cared so much in my life to see a similar level of frantic reflecting back at me. Because I'd never been as frantic as I was now. For a beat, I was frozen, almost stunned. She snapped me out of it when she slid her palms up under my shirt.

Oh hell yes. I needed more than seeing her breasts. I needed to feel her against me. I reached behind my neck and lifted my t-shirt up and over my head in one rough move. It fell to the floor beside hers. I stared down at her. Fuck. I'd been fantasizing about her breasts for too long. They strained against the black silk of her bra, her nipples taut little beads. I trailed a finger down between them before circling a nipple. It tightened under my touch. I could've lost myself in her breasts and gave in to the urge, cupping them in my hands, teasing her nipples with my thumbs, and savoring every breathy moan from her.

I couldn't say I meant to go slow because all thought had fled, but she made it near impossible when she rolled her hips against my cock.

"Dammit, Beck. Don't..."

Whatever she meant to say got lost in a low moan when I dipped my head and laved my tongue over the silk, wetting it and lightly scoring her nipples with my teeth. I alternated between her breasts, savoring the feel of her arching into me, the heavy weight of her breasts in my palms, and almost came in my jeans when she murmured my name.

That was how out of control she made me.

I flicked my thumb between her breasts,

and they tumbled free, the silk giving way. My memory of them from the brief moment in the showers didn't do them justice. They were round with dusky pink nipples, damp and taut from my attention. My heartbeat kicked up another notch, and my cock hardened even further. I was so hard, it was a miracle I didn't explode.

With a measure of control I had to force into action, I stepped back just as she reached for the buttons on my jeans. Because God help me, if she got her hands on me anytime soon, I'd lose what little control I had.

"You are so fucking gorgeous," I murmured, my eyes coasting over her.

She sat there on the counter, her thighs caging me, her lush breasts begging me to touch them again, and the soft curve of her belly yet another reminder she was all woman and more. Her hair was a rumpled mess, her curls falling around her shoulders. Her skin was flushed and just as I'd guessed, freckles were scattered randomly all over the place. I could spend hours making sure to lick and kiss every one, and maybe, just maybe that would satisfy my urge to taste her.

When my eyes landed on hers, I saw desire, surprise, and impatience reflected there.

My heart squeezed—a sensation so odd I didn't know what to make of it.

She moved suddenly, nudging me with her knee and sliding off of the counter.

"What are you..."

My question trailed off when she shimmied out of her jeans inside of a few seconds.

Oh. Well. That was quite all right with me.

She briefly lost her balance as she kicked her feet free. I steadied her, my hand landing on her hip. Excellent. I curled both hands on her hips and lifted her right back onto the counter. I was surprised to see she had on black silk panties to match her bra, which she was quickly shimmying free of her shoulders.

I meant to say something, something teasing and taunting. Before I could form a word, she dragged her palm roughly over my cock. Inside of a breath, she tore the buttons open and slid her hand inside my briefs, the zipper sliding down roughly on its own.

I groaned, my cock throbbing in her touch.

"Maisie..."

Damn. She stole my words again. They were lost in a hot jolt of lust.

Chapter Eleven

MAISIE

I looked up at Beck as I curled my hand around his cock, the skin hot and velvety. I wasn't the least surprised to discover he was quite the handful, literally. His gaze was fierce, the need contained within making me catch my breath. I should've been thinking more clearly—something, anything sensible —but I was far past that. The only thoughts tumbling through my mind were driven by the overwhelming need humming through me.

The moment I'd let the gates holding my desire back open, it had raced through me with such force, all I knew was what my body wanted. *Beck. Now.* I didn't care this was flat crazy, and I'd probably regret it. I'd even forgotten that I'd cast this net, thinking it likely reality wouldn't live up to fantasy. The opposite was turning out to be the case. I couldn't have fantasized the way it felt as if his gaze lit fires under my skin everywhere it landed, nor the heat spreading like wildfire through me, nor the sweet, tight pleasure coiling in my belly, the way my channel throbbed with nothing more than a look, the way my nipples tightened to an ache so acute and pleasurable when his teeth scored them. No, I couldn't have imagined any of this because imagination only goes so far when prior experiences don't even come close.

Being the loner I was, I'd tried my hand at dating here and there, but it was unsettling and annoying. Sex was best described as a letdown. I'd get turned on and hope for more, only to find myself rather ho-hum about it all.

This. Here. Now. *This* was far more than I'd imagined. The intensity of my need barreled through me with such force, I couldn't see past it. All I knew was what I wanted—to be closer to Beck, to have every inch of him bared to me and his cock, every generous inch of it, buried to the hilt inside of me. Maybe, just maybe that would slake my need.

The ache at the apex of my thighs grew. I

was hungry, greedy and needy, and I didn't give a damn. I didn't hold anything back and didn't even consider it.

"Fuck, Maisie," he muttered, his voice husky.

God, I loved his voice like that. He was always so suave, teasing and calculated. Right now, he didn't feel like that. He felt as wild and rough as I did.

I dropped kisses all over his chest. What a glorious chest it was. Beck shirtless was like a drug for my eyes. He was all hard planes. He wasn't the tidy fit you saw with guys who worked out all the time. He was lean, sinewy and hardened. You just knew he had this body because he'd earned it through the brutally hard work he did. A jagged scar ran along the bottom of his ribs on one side. I distantly wondered how he'd gotten it. I traced it with my tongue, all the while stroking his cock.

I felt the bead of pre-cum roll out of the head of his cock. I swirled my thumb in it and lifted my head. I drew the end of my thumb in my mouth and looked up at him. The salty tang was just a hint, but it sent a shiver through me.

His features were tense, locked to me. I drew my thumb out and meant to dip my head because I wanted more than that small taste. He laced a hand in my hair and roughly tugged me up.

"Hey..."

My protest was drowned out in his kiss. I wasn't protesting him roughly yanking me up. Not at all. My need was so great, everything was another domino in the cascade of pleasure barreling inside of me. I was only protesting that I hadn't gotten to take his rather magnificent cock in my mouth. That would have to wait for later. All thought got lost in the flood of sensation washing through me. Our kiss was wild, wet and messy. When he finally drew back, I sucked in a breath, nearly dizzy with need. I needed him more than air just now—or so it felt.

His lips blazed a wet trail down my neck as he reached between us, dragging his fingers over the wet silk between my thighs. I moaned, my hips rolling into his touch.

I was drenched, nearly quivering with need for him. He closed his teeth over a nipple, the sharp sensation sending an arrow of pleasure through me. I cried out, arching into him.

"My God, Maisie," he muttered, the feel of his breath on my skin sending shivers chasing in its wake.

He lifted his head, dragging his fingers back and forth over my panties, every pass making the ache there grow.

"You're so wet," he said, his voice almost reverent.

I flexed into him when he pushed my panties aside and sank a finger in my channel. I almost came right then. That's how close I was. Everything tightened inside.

My hips bucked against him. "Beck, please…"

My plea disappeared in the long moan that came when he added another finger and started stroking, slowly fucking me with his fingers. It wasn't enough though. I needed more. I reached for his cock, sliding my palm around it. In a flash, he drew back, fumbling in his pocket. He flung his wallet aside as he snagged a condom.

I wasn't prone to praying, but I thanked God right then he was quick and smooth. He had that condom on inside of a second. I curled my legs around his hips, my breath coming in ragged heaves. He held still, the tip of his cock resting in my entrance. My pussy clenched. I was near frantic to have him inside of me. I needed the stretch, to feel full, and I needed it now.

"Maisie."

My name fell into the quiet. I looked up to find his intent gaze waiting for me.

I swallowed, my chest suddenly tight. I couldn't say what I'd expected because I sure as hell never expected this to happen, but I certainly didn't expect the feeling between us. Oh, most of this was driven by the rampaging desire between us, but underneath it ran a sense of connection, of intimacy. I wanted to look away because it startled me, but I couldn't.

"Yes?"

"I suppose it might be too late, but I have to ask if you're sure about this."

Oh hell. I felt even more closely linked to him the second his words sank in. He just had to go and be all respectful. Well, as respectful as a man can be when we'd been making out as if our lives depended on it. He was there, his cock rock hard and kissing the heat of my core, but I knew he'd stop if I asked. Which only made me want him even more.

"Yes, God yes," I managed with a jerky nod.

He was still for another few beats, his dark green gaze searching mine. Never breaking eye contact, in one swift surge he filled me. The relief was so great, I cried out.

It was a tight fit, the delicious stretch of his cock so intense, I almost came from that alone.

He held still for a beat before easing his hand out of my hair and sliding both hands down to grip my hips. He began to move, a slow, steady rhythm of strokes into me. I was restless and frantic, chasing after the sweet release I'd been so close to the moment he'd touched me. His strokes were measured and controlled, while I wanted wild and reckless. I curled my legs around his hips, nipped along his neck, savoring the salty tang of his skin, and rocked into him.

I was ablaze inside, pleasure coiling tighter and tighter. Our skin was damp, slapping together with every thrust of his hips. I loved the way his fingers dug into my skin, I craved the rough touch, anything to push me higher and higher. The crescendo of pleasure rose higher and higher until I distantly heard my voice murmuring his name in between moans and rough gasps. He reached between us, pressing his thumb against my clit, so slippery wet with my need.

Just that subtle pressure and the crescendo reached its peak, pleasure roaring through me so hard and fast, it was dizzying.

My channel throbbed around him as I

tried to catch my breath. I felt him go rigid and sink deeply, his cock pulsing inside of me. His head fell against my shoulder, his breath gusting against my skin.

We remained like that—him standing in the cradle of my hips, his head bowed against me—for long moments with nothing but the sound of our breath gradually slowing in the room. I eventually dragged my eyes open, consciousness filtering in. One hand was laced in his hair, the other curled around his waist. I was holding on as if I never wanted to let go. I wasn't sure I did. So much for fantasy being better than reality.

Fantasy – 0.

Reality – 1.

Chapter Twelve

BECK

I held the fire hose and aimed it at the giant brush fire in the field behind the station. The water came out in a strong gush, hitting the flames flashing high. Somehow I'd ended up volunteering to do the annual training day we held for high school students. Normally, I helped out, but I didn't usually run the whole damn thing. We'd been in the middle of our weekly station meeting when the topic came up. Maisie had been sitting beside Chief Masters and ended up looking my way right when he asked who might want to run it this year since he'd be out of town.

With her liquid brown eyes on me, I'd inanely raised my hand. Truth was, I had no fucking idea what the chief had said at the moment. That's all she had to do was look at me now, and my brain turned to mush. So here I was, helping a bunch of high school kids put out a giant fire. We had a field behind the station where we allowed controlled burns whenever locals needed to deal with extra brush and the conditions were safe. We put a call out for anyone to drop off what they wanted burned, and we burned it. We went over all the main points of fire safety and how to determine when conditions were safe to burn and the like. Then, we let the kids light the brush pile on fire.

I actually enjoyed it for the most part, but ever since last week, I'd been nothing but distracted. Maisie had effectively blown my mind. I truly hadn't expected her to go for it. I'd figured I'd tease and hoped I could talk her into getting nice and naughty with me. I sure as hell hadn't expected her to fuck me senseless. A full week had passed, and she'd done a remarkable job of making sure she was never alone with me at the station. I tried texting and got polite replies, nothing more.

Meanwhile, I was about out of my mind with need. I was so bad off, I'd stopped by Wildlands the other night. I'd figured if Maisie wasn't going to let anything happen again, I'd best move on and get back into the swing of things. I was certain I'd see a woman, perhaps two or three, who were beautiful and down for nothing more than a good time. Yet, for the life of me, I couldn't do it. I hadn't the slightest interest. I wanted Maisie. No, I *needed* Maisie. She'd nearly ruined me for anyone else, and I had no fucking idea what to do about it.

I focused my attention back on the fire. Four teens had volunteered to help with this —three boys and a girl. I scanned the firebreak around the burning brush pile. We had a good twenty feet of wet ground around it. The wind was low today, as such it was a remarkably safe time to burn. I saw the girl struggling a little to manage her grip on the fire hose. I turned mine off and circled over to her.

"Need a little help?"

The girl adjusted her baseball cap with one hand and glanced my way, promptly sending a spray of water on the guy nearby.

"Hey! Watch out, Hailey," the guy said.

Hailey flicked her eyes from me to him, her gaze narrowing. "Oh shut up. It was an accident. You already soaked me, Danny," she said, gesturing to her water splattered jeans.

Danny rolled his eyes and shrugged.

Danny was lanky, his arms and legs ahead of the rest of him. "I was just joking," he countered.

Hailey's cheeks flushed. For a flash, she reminded me of Maisie. She had that same prickly exterior, yet she was pretty with her honey-blonde hair and wide brown eyes. I'd bet Danny liked her and, being as idiotic as most teen guys were, he thought spraying her with water would somehow be amusing to her. Definitely not.

Hailey dropped her hand and wrestled the fire hose back toward the fire itself.

"Fine, well I didn't mean to get you wet," she huffed toward Danny.

I caught Danny's eyes and offered a mildly sympathetic shrug before turning back to Hailey.

"Hold it like this," I said, gesturing to where she should place her hands and for her to use her hips to help her steady it.

Hailey watched me and promptly did as I said. She looked surprised after a moment. "Oh, that's much better."

"Yeah, when it comes to putting out fires, we need all the water pressure we can get. You get used to it. Plus, putting out fires by hand like this doesn't happen too often. Usually, we get hoses positioned and let the stands do the work for us."

Hailey chewed on her bottom lip. I glanced Danny's way and noticed he was still watching her. I didn't imagine Hailey would be an easy girl to like in high school. In this brief interaction, it was clear she was strong-willed and didn't care too much for unwanted attention.

"I came today because this is what I want to do," she said when I glanced back to her.

"You want to be a firefighter?"

She nodded firmly, her gaze determined. "Uh huh. And not just a firefighter, but a hot-shot firefighter.

"Ah, well, seeing as that's what I do, I'd say it's a good goal."

"Hailey, are you out of your mind?"

Danny's question came over my shoulder. Before I could say a word, Hailey's eyes narrowed, all but shooting flames at Danny.

"No! I'm not out of my mind. At least I have a goal," she retorted.

Danny stared at her and shook his head. "It's crazy hard and not many women can even make it through training." He caught my eyes. "It's what I want to do too, but I keep telling her it's harder for women."

Wow. This kid was giving a textbook lesson on how to piss a girl off.

"Oh shut up, Danny! So what if it's hard?"

At that moment, Susannah Gilmore walked up. Susannah was the one and only female hotshot firefighter amongst the crews here. She wasn't on my crew, but I knew her well enough to know she kicked ass out in the field.

"Susannah, perfect timing," I said by way of greeting.

She paused beside me, her strawberry blonde hair tucked up under a baseball cap and her blue eyes twinkling. Susannah was quite pretty, yet there was no spark between us. We were friends and nothing more.

"Why is that?" she asked.

"Hailey and Danny both want to be hotshot firefighters. Danny doesn't seem to think it's a wise plan for Hailey," I explained, throwing Danny to the wolves.

I figured if he was ever going to figure out how *not* to piss Hailey off, it might as well be now.

Susannah's twinkle faded to a sharp look when she glanced Danny's way. I left her to defend Hailey and meandered off. It crossed my mind that I probably wouldn't like it so much if Maisie ever put herself in the kind of danger I did on a regular basis.

Hours later, I wrapped a towel around my waist and snagged a cup of coffee on my way past the coffee pot to my locker. Willow Brook Fire & Rescue had landed a generous federal grant a few years ago, in large part due to the fact we housed three fully staffed hotshot crews that served wherever we were called in the United States. As such, that grant had given us a modernized, well-equipped station. Our showers were high end, and our locker room was spacious with plenty of room for our gear and a few changes of clothes. I tossed my towel in the hamper by the door as I passed by. I was the last person here this evening. Cade's crew had taken a call to a fire on the outskirts of town. Anyone else left behind earlier had helped me put everything away after our volunteer day ended and then taken off.

I swung the door to my locker open and had my briefs halfway up my hips when I heard a squeak. I spun around to see the back of Maisie. Her hips swung and her curly ponytail bounced as she all but ran away. Oh perfect. I had no idea she was still around.

My cock was instantly hard. I yanked my briefs up and followed her.

"No need to run, Maisie," I called as I stepped through the open doorway into the wide hallway that led to the front.

She came to an abrupt stop, but she didn't turn to face me. Oh good. I could give her a little grief over it.

I strolled toward her, not giving a damn that if she did bother to turn around, it was beyond obvious I was hard for her. I stopped when I was close enough to reach out and touch her. It was an act of pure will to keep myself from touching her, but I didn't. I had a few cards to play, and I intended to play them well.

"You've been avoiding me," I said, my voice coming out gruffer than I meant.

Hell, Maisie just snatched my control from me whenever she was near. It had been bad before, but now that I knew what it was like to be skin to skin with her... Well, it was safe to say my control was frayed to its breaking point.

She spun around, her dark eyes flashing.

Excellent. I loved it when she was flustered and annoyed with me.

Only problem. Now my cock was so hard, it ached.

"I have not!"

Damn, she was glorious. Her hair was in a

messy ponytail with wild curls escaping at will and her cheeks were flushed pink. She wore these stretchy black leggings and an oversized t-shirt that hung to her hips. Even with the t-shirt doing its damnedest to hide her assets, it was a losing battle. Her generous breasts pressed against the thin cotton.

"I say you have," I countered.

She crossed her arms and huffed, actually huffed.

"Why do you say that?"

I lifted a hand, holding my forefinger up. "Until right now, you've managed never to be alone with me for an entire week." I lifted another finger. "Your replies to my texts aren't even related to what I say." Another finger went up. "You won't look me in the eye." Another finger. "And, I say you're trying to pretend like nothing happened."

Her eyes narrowed, and she snagged her bottom lip in her teeth, worrying it. Oh hell. She needed to stop that. I'd finally gotten the upper hand for a second. As much as it was possible for me to have the upper hand while I stood there in my briefs and nothing else with a raging hard-on for all the world to see. Thank fuck only Maisie was here to see it.

"You promised not to say anything," she finally said.

"I haven't said anything to anyone, and I won't. But I sure as hell didn't promise not to talk to you about it."

She kept her bottom lip caught in her teeth as she stared at me. Uncrossing her arms, she rested one hand on her hip. "There's no need for us to talk about it."

Oh hell no. I wasn't letting her pretend like there was nothing between us. Not with lust drumming inside of me, and the air around us nearly vibrating with the force of desire.

"Well, we don't have to talk. There are other ways to communicate," I said slowly, dragging my words out.

I could see the tight little points of her nipples through her shirt. My cock throbbed.

Her cheeks went from pink to cherry red. I was close enough to see the jump of her pulse in her neck. It took all I had to keep from leaning over and dragging my tongue along the sensitive skin of her neck.

"Beck..." She paused and took a deep breath. "Look, I just don't think it's a good idea for anything else to happen. We work together, and you're sort of my boss. It was great and all..."

She stopped and shook her head in frustration. "This is all fun and games for you.

Like everything is. I need this job, and I don't want it to get weird."

I stared at her. Rationally, I knew what she said made sense. I filed it away to ponder later. But I didn't like it. I wanted her. Hell, I wanted her now more than I'd wanted her before.

"It won't get weird. It's not weird now, is it?" I countered.

Her teeth sank into her plump bottom lip again. For God's sake. I couldn't take it. I was trying to be a gentleman here and not just tackle her.

"You need to stop that," I said, my tone gruff and bordering on demanding.

Her eyes narrowed again. "Stop what?" she asked, her tone quite clearly annoyed.

"Biting your lip."

She stopped, if only because her mouth fell open.

"What is wrong with you?" she asked, her tone exasperated.

I decided to be entirely direct. No sense in dancing around my point.

"I want to kiss you. You do that, and it makes me want to kiss you more. You gotta give me some credit for holding back here. It's not like you can't tell what I want."

Her breath drew in sharply.

Good.

She slowly closed her mouth, staring at me. I didn't doubt she wanted me, but she was thinking. Way too hard. I needed to put a stop to that. I started to reach for her, but she stepped back.

"Beck, I'm not going to be silly and act like it wouldn't be fun to let things keep going with you. But it's not a good idea, and you know it. I don't want to be just another one of your fly-by flings. It's just not who I am." She paused, her gaze uncertain but determined.

I don't know what she meant to say next, but I jumped in to fill the gap and startled the hell out of myself.

"Maisie, you know damn well I don't think about you like that. You're the furthest thing from a fling. If that's what's in the way, stop thinking like that."

Maisie stared at me. I scrambled for purchase in my mind. I couldn't quite believe what I'd just said. As we stood there in the loaded quiet, I considered what to say next. My heart banged against my ribs, and a slight sense of panic tightened my chest and rose in my throat.

"If I'm not a fling, what am I?" she asked.

Excellent question. If only I had the answer.

I appeared to be on a roll with being honest, so my next comment hewed to that track.

"I don't know."

Her chocolate brown eyes just kept staring at me, questioning, assessing and with a hint of confusion layered in their depths.

I hadn't planned any of this. All I knew was I wanted Maisie. That need had overridden my usual control. I hadn't thought past what it might mean, the questions she might have, and the questions I now had. The only point of clarity was that I still wanted her. Fiercely. I shoved my own thoughts to the back of my mind because, honestly, I didn't know what to do with them right now. I had genuinely expected that once would be enough. I'd get Maisie out of my system, and we'd move on as friends. Hell, I'd never had trouble staying friends with women I previously dated. Yet, no one I'd dated was quite like Maisie. No one got to me the way she did. And that was before I had a taste of what it was like to be with her.

On uncertain ground, I fell back on the mundane. "What are you doing here anyway? I thought you left hours ago."

I felt rather foolish still standing there in my briefs. Although thank fucking God my cock wasn't so hard. Attempting to have a rational conversation about the state of whatever our affairs were had cooled the lust humming through me.

At my question, Maisie twisted a loose curl around the end of her finger. That was a nervous habit of hers. Even when her hair was pulled back, she certainly had plenty of curls to twist. They were wild. Then she went and bit her lip again. Oh hell. Just when I thought I was getting things under control.

"I came back to try to change the oil on my truck," she explained.

My confusion must have shown on my face.

Twirling that dark curl around her finger, she eyed me. "Susannah showed me how to change it. I thought I got it right, but I noticed there's an oil stain where I park the truck at Gram's house."

"Oh, well, wheel it in. Let me take a look."

She looked so damn relieved, it made me want to hug her. Only Maisie elicited this wanting-to-hug feeling in me. I wasn't much for the cuddly kind of affection. She also made me feel ten feet tall. Considering I wanted her like mad, it was a small favor to have her make me feel like a big man for a few minutes. All because I'd offered to help her change the oil. Man stuff.

"You'd help?" she asked.

It was then I realized I could bargain.

"Let's make a deal."

The relief in her eyes morphed into suspicion.

"What?"

"I'll check out your truck and fix whatever's wrong if you'll stop pretending there's nothing between us."

Talk about loaded silence. Damn. She stared at me, her gaze considering. I thought for a moment she was going to call my bluff. Because the truth was I'd take care of her truck no matter what. I figured she knew me well enough to know that.

Just when I thought I pushed too far, she spoke.

"Fine."

That's all she said.

"Fine?" I asked.

Her breath came out in a little huff. Damn, I loved annoying her. Of course, the side effect was I got hard all over again.

"Just that. Fine. I appreciate your help, and I'll try to..." She paused and gave her hand a little wave. "... I guess, not act like there's nothing there. I don't really know what that means, but I'll stop worrying about it for now."

I sent up a silent hallelujah. I wasn't about to reveal how fucking relieved I was.

"Deal then. I'll get dressed, and you can bring your truck into the side bay."

For a flash, I considered pushing the issue with her right now. We were alone, and I was already half naked. But I sensed I needed to play my cards right, and that probably meant giving her a little space. I didn't think about the fact that I was flat out crazy here. I was not the guy that proposed anything other than a fling. Yet, I couldn't even tolerate the idea of not having more of Maisie.

Chapter Thirteen

MAISIE

I stared down at Beck's boots. They were sticking out from under my truck as he checked out the situation with my oil filter. Battered, worn black leather boots was all they were. Yet, they were somehow part of everything he was. He was so casually masculine, I doubted he ever thought about it. Coming from California, I'd seen plenty of brand-spanking new leather boots made to look as if they were worn. I doubted those kinds of boots were even sold here in Alaska. Vanity wasn't much of a thing around here. I'd guess Beck probably blew through several pairs of boots like this every year.

He was rough, rugged, and so quintessentially alpha man, it was almost ridiculous. He shouldn't get to me the way he did. I mean, guys like him surrounded me day in and day out at the station. All tough as nails, hardened hotshot firefighters. Only Beck sent my belly into somersaults. Only Beck made me practically melt inside at how hot he was.

The first time I saw Beck, my pulse had lunged, flutters had spun in my belly, and he'd made me want things that weren't the least bit sensible.

I stared down at his boots, my mind spinning back to last week. I couldn't even think about it without getting all hot and bothered. My sex clenched right here where I stood. All of this was happening in my body while Beck was changing my oil filter. He appeared to talk to himself a bit when he worked because I occasionally heard him say something, but I couldn't make out what he meant.

My body recalled the feel of him filling me, the push and pull as he stroked into my channel. I swallowed against the tide of need rolling through me. This was insanity. I'd tried so hard all week to forget what had transpired. I'd scrupulously avoided being alone with Beck, which had taken some effort when he popped out front to chat. I'd never considered how often he did that and how much I liked it. He'd invariably say something to needle me, and we'd spar about something. All this time, I thought he annoyed me. He did, but it was fun and lighthearted. For the entire week since he'd left me boneless and shown me the folly of my belief that fantasy would trump reality, I'd pretended I'd been on the phone several times a day when he sauntered out front.

I wondered how long I could keep that up. I also wondered how long I could resist him. I'd fully expected us to have a one-night stand. I'd expected to leave slightly disappointed and easily expected to stop fantasizing about him. Instead, he'd blown my mind, sent me flying into an explosive climax and left me wanting more, more, and more.

I jumped when he slid swiftly out from under my truck. He was on his back on one of those rolling backboards. He flattened one boot to the floor, somehow managing to look as if he were lounging on the damn thing. A thin strip of his bronzed skin showed where his t-shirt rode up slightly above his jeans. That one little glimpse sent another wash of heat rolling through me. I knew just how hard and muscled he was and how he felt against me.

"All set," he announced with a quick grin.

"Oh, that's it? What was wrong?"

He rolled the backboard slightly and stood, catching the end of it with one boot. "Not much. You got it right. It just needed tightening. Since it was leaking, I went ahead and replaced the filter because the seal was a mess."

He quickly picked up a few tools and cleaned up. I watched while he washed his hands in the giant sink in the corner. We were standing between my truck and the garage wall. The side bay we were in was left empty unless they needed to bring one of the vehicles in for maintenance. Beyond us and closer to the main part of the station were the main bays, which contained two fire trucks. Aside from where we were, the garage was shadowy.

It was barely light outside with the sun's long, slow descent almost over. Through the window, I could see the thinnest sliver of its orb falling behind the mountains. The light was silvery gray outside.

I looked back toward Beck. He tossed a paper towel in the trash beside the sink and spun to face me, hooking his hands over the edge of the sink. It was bad enough how my body behaved when one of us was occupied, but it was downright embarrassing when there was nothing to distract me. The second his dark green gaze landed on me, my belly executed a slow flip and my pulse quickened. He was quiet, his gaze considering. In the narrow space between my truck and the sink, we were perhaps a foot apart. The space felt suddenly crowded and hot. I was burning up, inside and out.

Beck reached out and hooked his hand on the hem of my t-shirt. I'd returned to the station, expecting to see no one around. As such, I was wearing a t-shirt that hung past my hips and a pair of leggings, my usual comfy home outfit. I didn't feel the least bit sexy, but when Beck looked at me, my body lit up. He gently tugged me to him.

It would have taken a monumental effort for me to resist when every fiber of me wanted to latch onto him. I'd already forgotten the long list of reasons why I shouldn't let anything happen with him again. He pulled me flush against him and let out a satisfied hum.

I felt soft against him, if only for the contrast to his hardness. Aside from the fact I could feel his cock hot and hard against me, he was hard all over. My body almost sagged in relief against him. The effort it had taken to try not to notice him this past week had been more than I imagined. To let go into what I wanted—in short, to essentially bind myself to his body and forget the rest of the world—was such a release. I was humming with need, but for the moment, I wasn't fighting it. I closed my eyes and tried to catch my breath. While I was relieved to finally stop my internal fighting with my own desire, touching him only sent the need notching up.

"Maisie."

Beck's voice was low and taut. The sound alone sent a prickle of sensation down my spine. I opened my eyes. One look into his, and my breath and heartbeat got choppy. His gaze was fierce and so intent, I could hardly bear it.

I sucked in a breath. "Yes?"

"Is this when you tell me we can't do this?"

My head was shaking before I could form a reply.

"You'll need to be more clear," he said as he slid one hand around to cup my bottom while he lifted the other and trailed the backs of his fingers across my nipples.

They were already tight and achy, begging

for his touch. The subtle brush across the thin cotton almost made me moan. I scrambled for some semblance of control, my mind hazy with need. "Clear?" I choked out.

"You shook your head. I don't know if that means we can't do this, or if that means you're not saying we can't do this. How about you tell me what you want?"

He appeared to have more capacity for speech than I did, although his voice was gruff. I could feel the hard thump of his heartbeat against me. His cock was nestled at the apex of my thighs, right where he'd tugged me tight against him. I wished he wasn't demanding I make it explicit what I wanted. Somehow that made it feel real, something I couldn't chalk up to a wild, impulsive choice.

I looked into his eyes—fiery heat sliding through my veins and pooling in my belly, feeling the slick moisture between my thighs—and felt a depth of connection I'd never before known. It made me want to look away, but if there was one thing I wasn't, it was a coward. I was downright stubborn when it came to facing things head on. So I held his gaze with my heart beating like the wings of a bird and emotion tightening my throat.

I gulped in air and barreled through the fear chasing me inside. "I want you."

My words came out husky, roughened with the depth of my need. For good measure, I slid my palm over his cock. His lids fell as he arched subtly into my touch.

"Fuck, Maisie. You make me crazy."

"Well, at least that's two of us then."

His low chuckle sent shivers over my skin.

His fingers sank into my bottom. With a growl, he dipped his head and dragged his tongue along the side of my neck.

"You taste so fucking good," he murmured between licks, kisses and nips.

I'd gone from humming with need to nearly melting into a puddle. Thank God Beck had a firm hold on me. His lips finally made their way to mine. I needed to kiss him about as much as I needed to breathe and possibly more. I fisted a hand in his shirt and dove into our kiss. There were kisses and then there were Beck's kisses. Perhaps I was short on experience, but damn if he wasn't a pass master at it. Deep strokes of his tongue interspersed with tracing my lips, catching my bottom lip in his teeth, murmuring what I didn't know and then diving back into my mouth. It was the perfect balance of hard and soft, hot, deep, wet and overpowering. By the time he drew back, I was all but riding his knee, which had slid between my thighs somewhere along the way. My shirt was shoved halfway up and he had both hands cupping my breasts, his fingers teasing my nipples to madness.

Chapter Fourteen

BECK

I drew back and sucked in a breath. I was all but lost in the maelstrom of Maisie. Her lips were damp and swollen from our kiss, her eyes hazy and dark, and her skin flushed all over. Her hips were rolling against my thigh and I was so fucking hard, I thought I might explode.

I was normally more measured when it came to sex. I loved it and definitely loved making a woman go wild. Yet, it was all about the end game. With Maisie, it was something else altogether. Oh, it was want, it was need, but it was far more than that. There was no end game. I got lost in nothing but the sensation of being with her—having her full breasts fill my hands, her tight nipples rolling under my thumbs, the damp heat of her sex pressing against my thigh. There was nothing measured about anything I did with her. It was pure, raw, unfiltered lust mingled with something else. Something I didn't quite want to think about just now.

I lifted her against me and couldn't help the grin of satisfaction when she curled her legs around my hips. She was a bundle of lush, soft curves. Her musky scent surrounded me. Damn. Just the scent of her made me harder. I carried her around to the end of the truck bed, adjusted her in my arms and opened it with one hand.

"What are you...?"

Her question ended in a gasp when I slid her hips onto the back of the truck and reached between her thighs to drag my fingers over the damp cotton.

"You are so fucking wet," I murmured.

A little moan came from her when I deepened the pressure and passed over her clit.

I was about out of my mind, but I had a goal. I reluctantly moved my hand away and reached for the waistband of her leggings. She was quite helpful and swatted my hands out of the way to shimmy out of her leggings in no time. She was busy with me next, shoving my shirt up. It got caught, and she swore. I laughed and reached behind my neck to lift it off quickly. She started to unbutton my jeans, and I caught her hands in mine.

Her eyes flicked to mine, impatience contained in her gaze.

"Don't worry, we'll get there."

I snagged the hem of her t-shirt and lifted it off where it fell in a rumple to the floor with mine. Fuck me. She was glorious. Her breasts spilled out over the top of her black silk bra, the nipples taut little beads. Maybe this was only the second time we'd been together, but she appeared to have a penchant for black silk. It shouldn't have surprised me. She had a touch of goth to her look overall, but her creamy skin, her freckles and her general adorableness made it impossible for her to pull it off.

I flicked the tiny clasp between her breasts, groaning when they tumbled free. My mouth was on them before thought passed through. I *needed* to taste her, to feel her nipples tighten under my tongue and in my lips. She arched into me, crying out when I bit down lightly. I gripped her hips and tugged her to the end of the truck bed, her calves dangling around my hips. With her flexing against me, I mapped my way down her body, over the soft curve of her belly, and trailed kisses along the insides of her thighs.

She shifted restlessly against me when I pushed her thighs apart. The silk between them was soaking wet with her juices. I meant to drag this out, but I needed to see her. Hooking a finger over the thin edge of the silk, I dragged her panties off, slipping them into my pocket. I'd be damned if she went home with those on tonight. I looked down to see her pussy, pink and glistening. It distantly occurred to me she was too pure for where we were fucking. Oh, I didn't mean she was virginal. More that she was so fucking beautiful, so raw and so honest in how she responded to me. Where we were was most often filled with men coming back covered in soot. This place was all man, and she was all woman.

I slid my hands slowly up her thighs, pushing them further apart as I did. I dragged one finger through her folds—oh my fucking God, she was so wet. My knees almost buckled. Slick with her own juices, the scent of her was like a drug. I sank a finger knuckle deep inside of her, watching as her hips rolled into my touch.

"Beck, please don't make me wait," she murmured between breaths.

"Oh, I won't make you wait. This is round one."

I finally gave into what I wanted and let my tongue trace her cleft. Her hips bucked, and she gripped my hair. I added another finger into her channel and set to fucking her with my fingers while I tasted every inch of her. She was salty and sweet, and fucking glorious. She didn't hold back, and I loved that about her. She might be guarded and prickly, but her strong personality came through once she let down her guard.

With her hips rolling into me, I traced in and around her folds, grazing over her clit again and again, all the while stroking deeply into her channel. When she started to throb around me, I swirled my tongue around her clit and drew it into my mouth. She cried out sharply, my name following with a low moan, as she convulsed around me.

I drew back slowly, reluctant to create any space between us. I could've started with the same thing all over again, but she was already restless. She rose up on one elbow and reached for my jeans. My cock was so hard, I wouldn't have been surprised if my zipper was imprinted on it. She freed it inside of a second, while I barely had enough time to yank my wallet out of my back pocket and snag a condom.

She snatched it from me and tore the packet so hard I thought she'd tear the condom in half. I grabbed her hands. "Easy. I've only got one, so if you tear it, we're outta luck."

She huffed. "I need..."

"Oh, I need too," I said, almost growling the words. That got a laugh from her. "Let me do the rest."

I rolled that condom on in record time. I looked over at her, and my heart gave a swift kick. She was so damn amazing, she took my breath away. Her hair had come loose and fell in a tangled mass of curls around her shoulders. I was jealous of the few that rested against her breasts, teasing over her nipples. I didn't have enough hands to touch her everywhere I wanted to touch her. With her cheeks flushed, her generous curves, and those little freckles scattered in abandon all over her, she was the most beautiful woman I'd ever seen.

With need lashing at me like a whip, I positioned my cock at her entrance and sank inside in one swift surge. She was so wet, I slid in easily. She gasped a little and her eyes fell closed.

I didn't know why, but I needed her to look at me.

"Maisie."

Her liquid brown eyes opened. Once her gaze locked to mine, she didn't look away. I was so close to the edge, it's a miracle I hadn't come the second I sank into her creamy, tight clench. I held still for a beat and then began to move. With her legs curled around my hips, we rocked together. With her breath coming in rough, breathy pants, her eyes caught with mine, heat twisted at the base of my spine and my balls tightened.

I wanted her to fly with me. I started to reach between us, but she beat me to it. I was already out of my mind and driven by nothing other than the hottest, wildest need I'd ever experienced. The sight of her fingers circling over her plump and swollen clit snapped the thread of my control. My release hit me so hard, my knees buckled. I pounded inside of her so hard, I saw stars. I fell forward, catching her in my arms as I did.

The metal of the truck bed echoed with the force of my weight collapsing atop her. My head landed in the sweet curve of her neck. As I tried to catch my breath, her scent seeped into me. I felt her pulse kicking against my cheek. I lay still, absorbing the feel of her relaxed in my arms and thought to myself I could've stayed right there forever.

Chapter Fifteen

MAISIE

I skipped over a puddle and pushed through the door into Firehouse Café, the bell above jingling as I stepped through. I paused and glanced around. The place was packed. For the locals, good food and coffee were always here, so it was a central social gathering spot. In the summers, the place practically hummed with the addition of tourists. Throw in a rainy day and the tourists who would usually be outside hiking, biking, fishing, hunting or more were looking for somewhere dry to be.

Smack in the middle of Willow Brook on Main Street, Firehouse Café was housed in the town's original fire station. The tall square building had been renovated with the old garage turned into the seating area for dining and an open style bakery and kitchen towards the back. The fire pole in the center of the room was painted brightly with fire-weed flowers, in addition to bright colors and artwork throughout the café creating a whimsical and inviting space. The dining area was scattered with square wooden tables with a dining counter enclosing the mostly open kitchen and bakery toward the back.

I threaded through a cluster of tourists by the entrance and got in line. I'd been running late this morning and had forgotten to grab my lunch on the way out. I was starving, and I could seriously use some coffee. I'd had two nights of restless sleep. I couldn't get Beck out of my mind—day or night. Ever since our interlude in the garage, he'd taken up permanent residence in my mind and body. I almost laughed aloud. I'd now had the best sex of my life—twice—in a fire station, which also happened to be where I worked. That's how out of control I was with him. Nothing could hold me back once he touched me.

"What's so funny?"

I glanced behind me to find Lucy Caldwell sidling into line. Her blonde hair was pulled back in a slapdash ponytail and was as damp as mine was. Along with forgetting my lunch, I'd forgotten my raincoat this morning too.

I couldn't exactly tell her what I'd been thinking about, namely the fact I'd been pondering my sexual escapades with Beck at the fire station. God help me. So, I shrugged. "Oh nothing much. How are you?" I asked quickly, skipping right along.

"Starving. You?"

"Ditto."

Lucy's bright blue eyes caught mine. "Care to join me? We'll be fighting for a table as it is."

"Sure," I said.

It was a small thing really, but I wasn't used to it. My entire life before Willow Brook had consisted of bouncing from one town to the next. As such, making friends beyond the superficial hadn't been too easy. By the time I'd moved away from my dad, I was so busy scrambling to make ends meet and get myself through college, I hadn't had much time for socializing. Willow Brook was a welcoming place, yet I was still getting used to the fact I was here for more than a temporary stay. Susannah had only been nagging me about getting out and about more for about a year.

"Hey, hey Lucy," a man's voice said.

I glanced over to see Levi Phillips approaching. Levi was another firefighter. He worked on Cade's crew and also had plenty of women drooling over him. With his dark blonde hair, bright blue eyes, and the firefighter requisite body-to-die-for, he was certainly easy on the eyes. As usual, I felt nothing when I looked at him. Only Beck got to me.

Levi's gaze shifted to me. "Hey Maisie. Lunch break?"

I nodded. "You got it. Forgot to bring mine today."

The line inched forward, and Levi paused beside us as he took a long swallow from his cup of coffee. He appeared to be on his way out.

He hooked a hand in his pocket, his eyes flicking back to Lucy. When I glanced her way, she looked cranky.

"Did you forget how to say hello?" Levi asked, a slow grin curling his lips.

Lucy huffed a little. I wondered *what* her deal was.

"Hi Levi. How are you?" she asked, her tone cool.

Levi caught my eyes and winked.

"I'm right as rain. You?"

Lucy crossed her arms. "Fine. If you don't mind, Maisie and I were having lunch."

Our casual decision to eat together was suddenly a lunch date. Okay. I could go with that. I might not know what was going on, but if Lucy needed back up from me, she had it.

Levi arched a brow, his grin expanding. He simply shrugged. "Okay ladies. Have a nice lunch."

Lucy turned to face forward. I caught Levi's eyes, feeling a little bad about her blunt dismissal of him. Levi was a nice guy. He was always offering to help whenever anyone needed help with something around the station. I'd heard from the crew he was steady as a rock out in the field no matter how dicey things got.

Levi didn't appear to feel bad. He winked at me and shrugged. "Lucy doesn't appreciate being told she's gorgeous. That's my offense," he offered in explanation.

Lucy's breath hissed, and she spun back to him. She started to say something and then snapped her mouth shut. After a beat, she said coolly, "Have a nice afternoon, Levi."

He chuckled and kept on walking,

pushing through the door, the bell punctuating his departure with a cheery jingle. We finally reached the front of the line. I was wondering just why Lucy was so annoyed with Levi, but it was time to order food.

Janet James greeted us with a wide smile. "Hey girls, what'll it be today?"

Janet was the owner of Firehouse Café. She was almost always here. She'd been a good friend of Gram's. I remembered her stopping by Gram's house when I would visit when I was little. With her warm brown eyes, ready smile and motherly manner, she was easy to be around. She'd gone out of her way to welcome me when I came to see Gram before she passed away. She was also the one who'd dragged me down to meet with Gram's attorney. Without her, I might have left town already had it not been for the fact I was flat broke at the time.

"I need coffee as dark as you can make it for starters," I said.

Janet laughed. "Will a double shot in the dark do?"

"Perfect."

Oddly, I was a bit of a coffee snob—a side effect of working at a coffee shop in trendy San Francisco. Firehouse Café had damn good coffee, and Janet knew what I liked.

Two shots of espresso added to her house coffee might jolt my sleep-deprived brain.

"Lucy?" Janet asked.

"I'll take the same," Lucy replied quickly.

"Got it," Janet said as she spun away. "Go find a table. I'll bring your coffee over in a few and take the rest of your order then."

As luck would have it, a couple was leaving from a corner table. Lucy practically ran over there to snag it. I slipped into the chair across from her as she plunked down with a sigh.

"Levi Phillips annoys the hell out of me, " she announced.

"Kinda hard not to notice."

I didn't know her all that well yet, but since she was so direct about it, I figured it was safe for me to share my rather obvious observation.

Lucy tugged the elastic out of her hair and sifted her fingers through the damp locks. I wasn't going to comment, but Levi was right. She was beautiful. Her bright blonde hair fell in messy, damp waves around her shoulders. With her creamy skin, bright blue eyes and fine features, she was breathtaking. She was dressed in her usual construction gear with battered jeans streaked with dirt, a loose t-shirt, and leather work boots.

Lucy snapped the elastic on her wrist and met my eyes with a rueful grin. "Right. I guess I let him get to me."

"What's so annoying about him?" I asked, genuinely curious.

"He keeps trying to get me to go out to dinner with him," Lucy said, her cheeks flushing slightly.

I'd never have expected Lucy to get flustered over anything. She and Amelia were intimidating in their own right, what with holding their own in a male dominated field as the team that made up Kick A** Construction. After hearing her views on relationships last week over drinks and dinner, I was even more surprised. She'd reminded me of myself a bit—fairly certain worrying about relationships wasn't worth the bother.

I considered how to reply. My thoughts were that if she didn't feel anything for Levi, it probably shouldn't be a bother that he asked her out for dinner. Her reaction wasn't one of pure annoyance, as if he was pushing too hard. It was as if his attention made her too aware, and as a result, uncomfortable. My gut told me she was uncomfortable because she liked him. I didn't consider myself particularly astute when it came to stuff like this, but I knew what I saw because it was awfully close to how I felt about Beck.

Major difference: he'd fucked me senseless. Twice.

He was all I could think about most of the time. I was slightly relieved to have my attention focused on someone else's man problems.

"I suppose you don't want to go to dinner with him," I replied.

Lucy rolled her eyes and sighed. "Not really."

"Not really?"

Janet arrived at our table just then. She promptly handed us our coffees and pulled out her notepad. "Okay, what can I get you girls for lunch?"

"Give me whatever today's special is," Lucy said.

"Salmon burger and sweet potato fries?" Janet asked.

Lucy nodded firmly. "I'll eat anything you make, but thanks for letting me know what it is."

Janet chuckled and looked to me.

"I'll take the same."

"Well, that was easy," Janet said with a small laugh as she slipped her notepad back in the front pocket of her apron.

"When you gonna break down and go out with Levi?" she asked, flicking her eyes to Lucy with a sly grin.

Lucy was mid-sip with her coffee and sputtered. I handed her a napkin and stayed quiet. It didn't surprise me in the least Janet might nose her way in. Aside from Susannah, she was the closest friend I had around here. I chalked it up to her long friendship with Gram. She seemed to feel a sense of responsibility toward me. I'd already fended off plenty of questions from her about my non-existent personal life.

"Do you always eavesdrop?" Lucy asked. Her cheeks were bright pink as she glared at Janet.

Janet nodded. "Sure do. I can hear pretty much everything from anyone who's in line. Levi's been after you for months, and I don't know why you're putting him off. It's obvious you like him."

Lucy shook her head. "Relationships aren't my thing, Janet. How many times do I have to tell you that?"

Janet merely shrugged. "Suit yourself. I think you're wrong though."

Her perceptive gaze bounced between Lucy and me. "You two are peas in a pod.

Both all badass and all about being independent."

Blessedly, someone called Janet's name from the counter area. "Be back with your food in a bit," she said as she spun away.

Lucy caught my eyes and shook her head. "Oh my God. I love Janet, but she is the nosiest person I know."

"No argument from me there," I said with a laugh.

I took a gulp of my coffee, savoring its rich, bitter flavor. "Well, I'm no expert, but if *not really* means something other than just no, there's nothing wrong with dinner."

As soon as I said that, I wondered what the hell I was doing. Who was I to give anyone advice on dating?

Lucy stared at me, her cheeks still a little pink. After a beat, she sighed and idly traced the edge of her coffee cup. "Look, no matter what, relationships aren't my thing. Levi's nice and all, but anything close to dating is inviting disaster for me. I figure he'll eventually stop seeing me as some challenge he has to win and move on."

Her words made my heart twist a little. I didn't know her past and didn't know who put the pain and darkness I saw in her eyes, but it made me sad. I had my own good reasons for believing the single life made the most sense to me, yet here I was ready to tell Lucy, a woman who was just barely a friend, that maybe she should expand her horizons. It was sad to think she was cutting off that possibility for herself.

"Maybe. Or maybe not. I know Levi a bit since I see him around the station all the time. He's a pretty patient guy. Not that you're asking, but he's also nice. Like a few other guys, I know plenty of girls think he's hot, but he's not all cocky about it."

I could *not* believe what I'd just said. First off, I wasn't that close to Lucy. For all I knew, it would piss her off if I had anything to say about this. Just goes to show how underdeveloped my friendship skills were that I'd dive into this conversation at all. Here I was defending Levi who in many ways was so similar to Beck. Yet, he was one of the good guys. He might be hot and sexy and used to women falling all over him, but he wasn't a jerk. Something told me he liked Lucy for more than her looks.

That train of thought took a corner that led straight to Beck. I couldn't help but wonder if he really liked me, or if I was simply a challenge he needed to master. I shook the thought away. Not something I wanted to ponder just now. Or ever for that matter.

Lucy's cheeks went even pinker, and her mouth twisted. "Oh God. I was hoping I'd found a kindred spirit."

"Oh, I'm sorry, I..."

She waved my apology away. "Don't be sorry. Amelia's like the poster child for happily-ever-after these days. She used to be plenty bitter, but now her and Cade patched things up so nicely, it's almost nauseating to be around them. You're right anyway. I shouldn't let any of it get to me."

Janet spun by our table, quickly delivering our plates. "More coffee?"

I drained mine and nodded. "When you get to it."

She snagged my mug and kept moving.

Lucy and I settled in to eat. Conversation moved onto much easier territory. I left a while later after Lucy extracted a promise from me that I'd join her and Amelia at some girl's weekly card game they hosted.

My mind kept spinning back to Beck. My thoughts were a boomerang when it came to him. A few things could draw my attention away, but it always snapped back. Even though the conversation with Lucy had been about her, my heart felt a little funny about it all. The sadness I felt surprised me. It shouldn't. Why should I care she'd decided to wall herself off from any opportunity of a relationship? I supposed I did because it hit a little too close to home for me.

BECK

The sound of the helicopter blades rumbling through the air was oddly comforting. I leaned my head back against the seat with a sigh. I was bone tired and so was our entire crew. We'd been called out to a fire that just wouldn't fucking die in central Alaska. Our crew had finished a two week rotation before we'd been relieved by one of the crews from the Fairbanks area. We were in the midst of another dry summer, which was keeping hotshot crews all over the state busy. The spruce bark beetle had ravaged Alaska's massive swaths of evergreen forest. The beetle had found its way here via lumber shipments from Asia. Since its arrival, it had stayed busy surviving off of

Alaska's bountiful spruce trees and leaving nothing but acre upon acre of dead trees in its wake. Hot, dry summers and that much fuel for fires meant they burned fast, spread easily, and were damn challenging to put out.

I rolled my head to the side and watched the landscape underneath us. When I was deep in the wilderness fighting fires, it was easy to forget we were on sacred ground. Alaska's beauty was breathtaking. I watched the blackened sections of forest recede behind us. As we flew further south, the trees became thicker and greener and the Alaska Range unfolded ahead. Denali rose high in the sky, the pinnacle of the Alaska Range. Fluffy white clouds were arrayed around its peak.

My breath caught for a beat. It didn't matter I'd been born and raised in Alaska and its natural beauty was a part of my everyday existence, it still blew me away sometimes. My grandfather, long since passed away, used to refer to the wilderness as God's cathedral. He hadn't been a particularly religious man, yet he'd hewed to the belief we must respect the ground on which we walked. I took a slow breath and watched the mountains as we flew above them. The thin ribbon of a river glittered under the sun's rays. I scanned the horizon as I tracked the path of the river.

Willow Brook came into view, and Maisie, who'd been permanently parked in my brain for weeks, gave my heart a little nudge. When I was out working a fire, there wasn't much time to ponder. The metaphor that the days were long was no metaphor for hotshot firefighters in Alaska. The sun was up around four in the morning in the more northern part of the state where we'd been and didn't set fully until after midnight. A mere four hours at best was what constituted 'night' there during the summer. We'd worked dawn until dusk and collapsed every night. Only then, in those exhausted moments before I tumbled into dreamless sleep, did I have much time to think. What little thought I had saved up went to Maisie. I missed her. I'd never missed anyone when I was away.

The experience of the feeling itself was odd—odd enough it made me shift my shoulders and roll my neck just now. I wondered if she'd be on duty when we landed. She should. The fact I knew her schedule spoke volumes. Funny thing though was I'd known her schedule ever since she'd started working at Willow Brook Fire & Rescue. Right from the start, I'd looked forward to walking in and seeing her. I'd loved how she was so bitchy with all of us at first. She'd long ago moved past that, yet if I was honest, I went out of my way to provoke her because it was damn fun to rile her up. It also turned me on. Now that I'd had a taste of her, everything about her turned me on. Just thinking about the last time I'd seen her got me hard.

It had been the day after our last mind-blowing interlude in the garage. My crew had gotten the call out the following day. It was my job, and I was entirely accustomed to taking off for weeks at a time. Yet, I hadn't been able to keep myself from stopping by her desk. I don't know what I'd wanted, but I'd wanted more than what I got.

She'd reverted back to being cool with me. It rankled me. That itself was another layer. The way she was getting to me was its own conundrum. I was an easy come-easy go kind of guy. I'd walked into this thinking I'd get my out of control lust for Maisie under control. Instead, all kinds of unexpected side effects were barreling out of control. For starters, being with her had only sent my need for her into the danger zone. I'd always guessed she'd be bold and passionate because it suited her personality. That was how she was, no matter the particular emotion. I hadn't bargained on how much that would only pour fuel onto the fire of my need for her.

I shifted in my seat when the memory of her crying out and clenching around me filtered through my thoughts. Fuck. I was so screwed. I should've been freaking out about this. Yet, I wasn't. In fact, I'd pretty much convinced myself it was time to make a major play for her. This very thought should've given me pause. What the hell was I thinking? I was thinking Maisie was so fucking hot, all I wanted was more, more, and more. There was that and the way my heart twisted in my chest whenever I thought about her. I had no clue what to think about that because it was something I'd never experienced. All I knew was it fed straight into my desire and vice versa, both feelings feeding into each other.

The helicopter pilot said something into his headset and then angled our path toward the landing pad behind the fire station. Willow Brook had a tiny airport, like just about every town or village in Alaska. Thousands of small planes took flight across the massive state since much of it wasn't connected by the highway grid. The small airport in Willow Brook had a few plane hangars and not much else. Its small runway backed up to the fire station, which offered a convenient location for our helipad.

Once we landed, I climbed out along with the rest of the crew. Fred Banks, the pilot, clapped me on the shoulder when he handed me my gear. "Figure I'll see you in another few weeks, eh?"

His blue eyes crinkled at the corners in his weathered face when I glanced his way. Fred was tough as nails and looked it. With his steely gray hair, lithe build and ready smile, he was always a welcome sight at the end of a run out fighting a fire.

"Usually do, Fred. Where you headed next?" I asked in return.

"I'm shacking up here for the night, but tomorrow I head to Fairbanks. I've got a few flights booked out of there."

"Ah, well make sure to grab some good coffee at Firehouse Café before you fly out tomorrow."

Fred winked. "Wouldn't miss it. Janet fixes me up with a to-go lunch too."

I chuckled and gave a wave as I headed toward the station. "Of course she does. Until next time."

My stride picked up as I approached the station. Usually, I'd head straight for the showers, no pause along the way. Today, I needed to see Maisie first. I kicked the door open with my boot and turned into the hallway that led to the front. Another kick to another door, and there she was.

She sat behind the curved counter at her desk. Her wild curls were barely tamed into a ponytail. Her eyes whipped up from her computer screen. The second she saw me, her cheeks flushed. She might want to play it cool, but I didn't give a damn.

Chapter Seventeen

MAISIE

I stared at Beck and felt my cheeks go hot. He was wearing battered, faded jeans streaked with dirt and a gray t-shirt that did nothing to hide his ridiculously muscled chest and arms. His heavy gear bag fell to the floor with a thump. It took me a second to realize he was rounding the desk and coming straight for me. In a flash, he was beside me, his dark green gaze bearing into me.

My pulse lunged, my breath hitched, and heat flooded me. All he had to do was *look* at me and my sex clenched. He'd been gone two whole weeks, and I'd missed him. Terribly. My heart gave a resounding little kick to my ribs as I stared at him. His black curls were messy and windblown. He probably hadn't showered in days, if not for the entire time he'd been gone. I was using the term *shower* quite loosely. I knew perfectly well when the guys were out in the field, a shower meant perhaps a dip in a stream, or a splash bath if they had time to rest. Anyway, he was a rumpled mess, and I was so happy to see him, emotion clogged my throat.

I might have fantasized here and there about him when my defenses were down ever since I'd met him. Yet, I was accustomed to him being gone for stretches of time. That was the life of a hotshot firefighter. All of them rotated in and out of town for weeks at a time. I hadn't expected to miss him. Usually when Beck was gone, I experienced a bit of relief. He kept me on edge with his teasing, and I'd been so determined to keep my distance. When he was gone, I could relax and not worry about my body's disobedience.

Giving into my desire for him had turned me into a crazy person. As long as I didn't think about anything that had transpired between us, I was fine. The problem was I could hardly stop thinking about it now. My silly idea that fantasy would beat out reality had turned out to be so ridiculously wrong.

My eyes greedily soaked in the sight of him. He caught the back of my chair and spun me toward him. It was an act of will to keep from jumping up and throwing my arms around him.

Wow. This is how ridiculous you are over him. Get some kind of grip.

My little lecture did nothing to corral the need rampaging through me and the way my heart started skipping with joy to see him. I wouldn't say I didn't worry about the guys when they were out in the field. I knew they had a dangerous job, yet they were all so authoritatively capable that I rarely considered the true possibilities. These last two weeks while Beck was gone? More than once it had crossed my mind that he could get hurt, or die. Just last year, one of the crews had been in a plane crash. They'd all walked out with nothing more than minor injuries, but it could've been so much worse.

Beck startled me when he rested his hips against the half wall beside my desk and slid his back down the wall until he was rocking on his heels between my knees. He caught my hands just when the emergency line beeped in my ear.

With his gaze intent on me, I had to look away. He easily freed one of my hands, but held the other between both of his. I forced my attention off of him and tapped the button on my headset to take the call.

"911, what's your emergency?"

"Hi Maisie, it's Carrie Dodge."

I almost laughed. I'd come to learn that once people knew who I was, they tended to greet me by name when they called 911. I was the sole dispatcher for Willow Brook with Anchorage as our back up in off hours, so it stood to reason they'd do that. It still amused me. It also gave me a sense of belonging that felt strange.

"Hi Carrie, can you tell me the nature of your emergency?" I asked, sticking to the script for taking calls.

I remembered my last call with Carrie when it had taken her a good ten minutes to tell me she was trapped inside an excavator in a ditch. Beck idly traced his thumb across the back of my palm. The feel of the roughened pad of his thumb reminded me what his hands felt like in all kinds of other places. My channel clenched, and I roughly forced my attention off of that, shooting him a glare.

"Oh, Herman's stuck in that same tree again. Usually, I'd use the excavator and get him out with the bucket. It's been kind of a game for us. But if you remember, last time I did that, it didn't go so well."

"I do remember that. Do you mind if I ask if you're okay?"

I could hear her huff through the line and bit back a laugh.

"I'm fine. I just need someone to come get Herman out of the tree," she replied.

"You got it. I'll send one of the crews out your way."

"You're not gonna make me stay on the line and chat this time, are you?"

"No need this time. You're safe and sound. If one of the trucks isn't there within fifteen minutes, you can call me back, okay?"

The line clicked off without a reply. I shook my head and glanced down to Beck. My pulse lunged again and my heart felt funny. He sat propped against the wall, his eyes locked to me. The moment felt too intimate, too much, and I didn't know what to do with any of it. So, I focused on the practical.

"Hate to tell you this, but you might need to rally a few guys to head out to help Carrie Dodge get Herman out of a tree."

A dark brow rose in question. "Herman?"

"Her cat."

A low laugh rumbled out of him, and my belly spun, little sparks of heat scattering through me.

"Where are the other crews?"

"Cade's crew is out dealing with a fire at that construction site just outside of town, and the other crew went to Anchorage for a rotation. Cade's guys didn't leave until Fred called in your landing time. I suppose they guessed you guys could deal with any calls that came in."

Beck leaned his head back with a sigh. I'd been so focused on finally seeing him after missing him so much for two weeks, I hadn't noticed how tired he looked. Weariness etched his features. He lifted his head and nodded before squeezing my hand slightly and pushing himself to standing. He was quiet for a beat, his eyes coasting over my face.

"Can I see you tonight?" he asked, his voice gruff.

His question startled me, enough so that I was nodding before I thought about it.

The hot look in his eyes sent a jolt of heat through me. My God. The way he looked at me made me all kinds of crazy inside.

"You probably don't have to go out to Carrie's. Sounds like just enough guys with the cherry picker can probably handle it,' I said, referring to the buckets firefighters used to be lifted up to high locations.

Beck shrugged. "I know I could make someone else go, but that's shitty. We're all beat. The least I can do is help out."

My heart squeezed as I stared at him. He just had to go and be a decent guy. He was the superintendent of a crew of twenty. There was no doubt it would only take a few of them to help rescue Carrie's beloved Herman. But Beck wasn't the kind of leader who shirked duty and shifted it off on his crew when he could handle it. On another day when they weren't all worn from weeks fighting a wildfire, he might easily send a portion of the crew out and hang back. But not today.

I swallowed against the sudden emotion clogging my throat and nodded. "Right. Okay, well..."

My words trailed off because I had no idea what else to say.

He glanced at the clock above the door to the hallway beside my desk. "You leave at six?" he asked.

My schedule was the same whenever I was here, so it shouldn't surprise me he knew it. But still. A little curl of warmth wrapped around my heart to think he paid attention to anything to do with me.

"Uh huh," I replied, glancing at the clock

on my computer screen. I'd be finishing my shift inside of a half an hour.

"I'll go make sure Herman's okay," he said with a grin before he paused. "Then, I'll come to your place. How's that sound?"

Again, my head was just nodding along.

He stood there for a beat, his eyes on me. The air felt electric. I wanted all kinds of things—to touch him, to burrow into his strength. Yet, I did nothing because we were most certainly not somewhere private. An entire crew was in the station now, not to mention Chief Masters was still around somewhere. So I held my feelings at bay and watched as he winked and spun away.

Chapter Eighteen

BECK

Jesse Franklin flashed a grin as he handed over Carrie Dodge's cat. Herman eyed me as if he were annoyed with the entire matter. We had just spent a good hour maneuvering the cherry picker as he leapt from branch to branch in the tall spruce tree. Conveniently, Herman was an orange tabby cat. His bright fur helped us find him as he'd darted about in the upper branches of the tree.

I rubbed my knuckles under his chin, and he promptly set to purring.

Jesse chuckled. "Oh, now he's pleased. Damn good thing I had gloves on. He was scratching like crazy up there."

I looked down at Herman as he purred away and burrowed into my arms. "Let me drop this guy off, and we can head back to the station," I said, glancing up at Jesse.

"Got it."

I walked across the yard. Carrie was already walking toward me. I'd known Carrie since I was a kid. She seemed ageless to me. She had the same silvery hair pulled back into a long braid and sharp blue eyes that she'd had back when I was young. She moved a tad more slowly, but that's about it. She met me halfway, tut-tutting at Herman the moment I handed him over.

"You know better than to climb that high, Herman."

His purr rumbled a little louder as she glanced up at me. "Thank you for getting him down. This is the third time he's done that this summer."

I shrugged. "No problem. Usually I'd try to come up with some sort of suggestion for how to keep him out of that tree, but he's a cat."

Carrie laughed. "Exactly. Until last time, I took care of it myself. I just need to get my excavator..."

"You are *not* about to tell me you're getting it fixed and would be foolish enough to try to get him out with it again, are you? You know that's not exactly what it's for, right?"

Carrie shrugged. "What else am I gonna do with it? I only have it because John never got rid of it before he passed away," she said, referring to her deceased husband.

"Carrie, just call us. We'll come get Herman out of the damn tree whenever you need."

She sighed and glanced down at Herman who was entirely unrepentant and purring away in her arms. "Well, thank you. Do you boys need anything to eat?"

My mind flashed to Maisie, and I glanced at my watch. We'd been here longer than I planned, and it was well past six. "Nah, but thanks for the offer."

She waved from her front porch as Jesse and I drove away. I considered asking Jesse to drop me off at Maisie's as her place was on the way to the station, but that would open up a line of questioning I wasn't ready for. I was restless and impatient to get to her.

After the fastest shower of my life, I leapt in my truck and headed to her place. When there was no answer to my knock at the kitchen door, I carefully opened it, not patient enough to wait for her.

"Maisie?"

I heard a muffled voice and pushed the door open wider. I was greeted by the sight of her bent over as she looked inside the oven. Hot damn. Her bottom was displayed perfectly for me. The only downside was she wasn't naked yet. As it was, she wore stretchy leggings that were tight over her lush bottom. I beat back the urge to walk up behind her and run my hands over her hips. Aside from those few moments at the station, it had been a full two weeks since I'd seen her. I sure as hell didn't know where we stood. I knew what I wanted though—her. Like crazy.

She straightened and turned to face me. Her cheeks were flushed pink and her hair was down, those wild dark curls falling in a tumble around her shoulders. I wanted to walk up to her, bury my hand in them and pour two weeks of banked lust into her lips.

"Hey, I wasn't sure if you were still coming because..."

Apparently I wasn't thinking. At all. Because I did precisely what I imagined. I kicked the door shut behind me and was in front of her in two long strides. I slid a hand in her hair, the curls silky and soft. Her breath drew in sharply. I pulled her flush against me. My cock had gone hard the second I saw her. Sweet hell. Feeling her soft curves against me and the warm heat at the apex of her thighs, I groaned.

The air around us hummed to life. I closed my eyes and breathed in the scent of her. When I opened them, I found her chocolate brown gaze waiting for me. I could practically see questions spinning in her mind. I knew from the rapid flutter of her pulse in her neck and the flush on her cheeks that she wanted me. I sensed if we spoke, she'd start asking questions and I couldn't answer anything right now. I just needed...*her*.

I dipped my head and dropped kisses along her neck. I felt the goose bumps rise on her skin and felt a rush of satisfaction. I didn't want to be alone in my wild, thrumming need. A distant warning bell clanged in my mind, but I ignored it. I was many things, but getting lost in desire in any way other than light and casual wasn't something I did. Ever. But I didn't want to think about it. I just wanted to lose myself in Maisie and this thing between us.

A beeping sound intruded. I lifted my head to feel Maisie stepping back. In reflex, I followed her. I couldn't stop touching her. Not now.

She spun around and turned off the oven timer. Conveniently, she bent over and opened the oven to check on whatever she had in there. I ran my hands along the curves of her hips and couldn't resist cupping her bottom and sliding a hand between her thighs. I grinned when I heard a little moan escape from her. I dragged my fingers over the cotton there—it was damp. Just knowing she was wet made my cock so fucking hard, it ached.

"Turn the oven off," I said, my voice low and rough.

I drew my fingers in another pass over her pussy. She arched reflexively into my touch and glanced over her shoulder.

Damn. She had no artifice to her whatsoever, and she was the sexiest fucking woman I'd ever known. Hands down. Her bottom lip was snagged in her teeth. With a loose curl dangling over her cheek, she looked rumpled and wild, and I wanted her so badly, I ground my cock against her.

"When did you get so bossy?"

"Since I haven't seen you for two weeks too long. The five minutes at the station don't count. Turn the oven off," I repeated.

A grin curled the corner of her mouth before she turned away and reached up to turn the oven off. She straightened and closed it. All the while, I stayed flush against her, my cock throbbing with need. Once she turned in my arms, I slid a hand into her hair again and fit my mouth over hers. I poured two weeks of lust and longing into her mouth. She didn't hold back, not even an inch. Our kiss went wild inside of a second with our tongues tangling, our breath mingling and madness building inside of me.

I needed more. Now. I broke free and stared at her.

"Bedroom," I choked out.

She started to draw back and turn.

"Nope. Not close enough," I said as I caught her hand and tugged her back to me.

She glanced over her shoulder, her eyes disbelieving.

"I can't exactly get to the bedroom without, well, walking there," she explained.

"Sure you can."

I lifted her against me, grinning when her legs reflexively curled around my hips.

"You're carrying me? Wouldn't a piggy back ride be easier?" she asked, her tone droll.

I shrugged. "Maybe so, but this is how we're doing this. Tell me where to go."

She giggled, and my heart clenched.

Maisie didn't giggle often. She was too tense, and thinking about that made my heart ache a little. I wasn't used to worrying the way I did about Maisie. I suddenly wanted to know why she was so prickly and guarded and to tell her she didn't need to be that way. I wanted to take care of her and never see that slightly worried look that was so often present in her eyes.

She looked over her shoulder and pointed to the stairs that led upstairs. With her held close against me, I managed to make my way up the stairs. It was a damn miracle I didn't stumble on the way up once her lips got naughty with my neck. I wasn't accustomed to being on the receiving end of this kind of attention. Oh, don't get me wrong. I was plenty accustomed to blatant flirting and se-duction, yet now that I'd had a taste of Maisie, I'd discovered something new. There was nothing practiced or measured about her. It never felt as if anything was calculated to manufacture a response. Everything was so real and raw, it caught at my heart and fed into my own need like nothing before.

I cleared the top step with lust drumming through my body so hard and fast, I had to pause and drag my tongue along her neck. The taste of her wiped my mind clean of any-thing else.

"Bedroom," I murmured against her neck.

She lifted her head. I glanced around, taking in where we were. The balcony ran along the wall upstairs with a railing to the other side, overlooking the two stories of windows in the living room. The sun was at the end of its slow slide down the horizon, leaving a watercolor sky in its wake. She nudged me with her elbow.

"Here," she said softly, her voice husky.

I glanced to my other side to see the door where she was pointing. I turned and shouldered through it, adjusting her in my arms. Carrying her was a kind of heaven I hadn't imagined. She was a bundle of curves, and I loved having her held tight against me, the heat of her core rubbing against my cock. I didn't think much about the whole tough, strong guy thing, but damn it felt good to have her close in my arms, as if I could somehow protect her from anything.

We were in that in-between time of dusk where the light was wispy. The last rays of the sun fell through a window to one side of her bedroom, casting a soft glimmer in the silvery light. I glanced around, taking in the space. She had a low bed built into the wall with bookshelves on either side and pillows piled high. I faced a conundrum. I didn't want to let her go. At all. But I wanted her bare naked with me buried inside of her. To get from this point to that one, I would have no choice but to let her go.

I eased her down, reluctant to step back. She instantly distracted me by reaching for my belt. Before I knew it, she was shoving my jeans down around my hips and curling her palm around my cock. We were standing at the foot of her bed, and she settled her hips on the edge and glanced up.

I meant to say something. Hell if I know what. She promptly robbed me of the ability to speak when her tongue darted out and licked the drop of pre-cum off the head of my cock.

I groaned. God help me. I wasn't used to being at anyone's mercy, but with her wide brown eyes flicking up at me through her lashes and her tongue exploring every inch of my cock, my knees nearly buckled. I threaded my hands in her hair as she proceeded to drive me mad. Her tongue was far naughtier than I ever could have imagined. She dragged it in slow strokes up and down my shaft, teased the head of my cock with swirls and kisses, and finally, *finally*, closed her lips around my shaft.

Oh my fucking God. I was about out of my mind with need once the warm suction of her mouth started working on me. I was so close to release. Hell, it had been two full weeks since I'd had any. It was fair to say when you were a hotshot firefighter spending long days fighting fires, sex was far from your mind. There were also zero opportunities. I hadn't even jacked off in two weeks. So with her mouth driving me to the edge and need coiling so tightly inside of me, I almost let go.

When she drew back and glanced up at me, I caught the end of a frayed thread of control and stepped back. It was a damn miracle with her lips swollen and damp from her thorough attentions to my cock. She started to reach for me again, but I took another step back, snagging my shirt behind my head and throwing it to the floor. I needed to feel every inch of her against me.

I tugged her up, roughly yanking her t-shirt over her head and groaning at the sight of her full breasts barely contained inside a black silk bra. Fuck me. Her penchant for black silk was the icing on the best cake I'd ever had. She shimmied out of her leggings, while I kicked my boots and jeans off.

I was beyond frantic and just needed to get as close as physically possible to her as quickly as possible.

Hot lust whipped at me, driving me.

Nothing was measured, nothing was calculated.

In seconds, we were tangled up on her bed, her skin soft against me. I couldn't even remember if she'd taken her bra and panties off, or I had. All I knew was the sense of relief I felt when I stroked between her thighs and found her hot and slick.

I mapped her body with my lips and hands. Trailing kisses up her neck, savoring the tang of her skin, I murmured, "Missed you..."

My words just slipped out. I felt them echo somewhere in my heart. Maisie went still, and I could feel the rapid beat of her pulse under my lips. I lifted my head to find her eyes wide open.

I might not have been thinking when I spoke, but I meant it so fiercely, I didn't intend to back off. I admit it made me a little uncomfortable. I wasn't accustomed to any of the feelings Maisie elicited, but they were there, and I wasn't a coward.

My heart pounded, swift and hard, against my ribs. She stared at me in the weighted quiet.

"You missed me?" she asked in a husky whisper.

For a beat, I hesitated and wanted to shy away. Yet, I didn't.

"Yeah. I did. It was a long two weeks."

I waited, wondering if I'd spoken too soon. Maisie was skittish and prickly, a bit like a porcupine.

I watched the rich chocolate brown of her eyes flicker, the color shifting subtly like clouds drifting through the sky.

I could feel her tighten inside. She sucked in a breath of air, letting it out in a rough sigh. "I missed you too," she said, her words tinged with resignation.

I took it as a win and brushed her tangled curls away from her face. With need drumming inside of me, I shifted atop her. Her knees fell open, and her palm slid up my spine. My cock was nestled in her folds, so slick and wet, I almost sank inside of her right then. Reality nudged me in the nick of time. I didn't have a condom.

I started to draw back, but she curled her legs around my hips and held me in place.

"I hate to tell you this, but I don't have a condom. Usually I do, but I've been out for two weeks and..."

"Forget it. I'm on the pill."

I slid up on an elbow and looked at her.

Thoughts spun through my mind. I couldn't even recall the last time I'd had sex without a condom. You didn't get to be a hotshot firefighter without a mindset of preparation. Unexpected pregnancy didn't fall under preparation. Whatever she saw in my gaze, hers shifted from hazy and passionate to uncertain.

"I probably shouldn't have assumed... I just..."

I shook my head. "Stop. You just surprised me. That's all."

I knew what I wanted. Desperately. But she had to be sure.

"Are you sure?"

She nodded quickly. "Uh huh. I've been on the pill forever."

I didn't hesitate and shifted my hips back, sinking inside of her in one swift surge.

Her channel was tight and slick around me. It felt so fucking good, I almost came right then and there. I laced my fingers into hers and stretched her arms up, dusting kisses over her face and down along her neck as I struggled to latch onto my control.

She wasn't having that and starting rocking her hips against me, little breathy moans and pants coming from her. That did it. My control snapped, and I slid my hips back, sinking to the hilt again. Everything blurred into nothing but sensation. The feel of her breasts pressed against me, her nipples tight little beads, her skin damp against mine, her hips rising to meet every stroke of mine, her channel pulsing around my cock— so tight, hot and wet.

Heat twisted in my spine, tension bundling tighter and tighter until she arched into me, crying out my name. My release barreled through me so hard, my head spun as I spent myself inside of her.

I tried to shift my weight to her side, but she tightened her legs around me.

"Don't move," she murmured, her lips against my neck.

"I don't want to crush you," I said with a small laugh.

I eased carefully to her side, but stayed buried deep inside of her. Relief rolled through me. It wasn't simply the pure relief of finally finding a release valve for my pent up need. It was the relief of finally being tangled up skin to skin with Maisie again.

Chapter Nineteen

MAISIE

"911, what's your emergency?" I asked, scanning my computer screen as the system scouted for the caller's location.

Whether someone was calling from a cell phone or landline, the computer system instantly scanned to pinpoint the location. Before the person answered my question, the system told me they were calling from a cell phone and were located close to the main highway leading into Willow Brook because their signal pinged off of a cell tower beside the highway.

"Um, we had a car accident when we swerved to keep from hitting a moose," a woman said, her voice shaky.

I tapped the button that would alert the

crew on duty, which happened to be Beck's crew. About the only time I wasn't thinking about him, more accurately *obsessing* about him, was when I was taking calls. Then, my attention narrowed like a laser to the person on the line.

"Okay, we have a crew on the way. Can you tell me your name?"

"Jerri, it's Jerri."

"Okay, Jerri. I'm Maisie. Can you confirm your location for me?"

"We're on the highway outside of Willow Brook."

"Is anyone hurt?"

"Um, I think so, but I can't tell. When my husband swerved to avoid the moose, our camper hit a telephone pole and we rolled into a ditch. I'm smashed in the corner of the passenger side, and I can't see very well."

Jerri's voice was shaky, and I could feel her fear and worry vibrating through the phone line.

I heard the siren of the ambulance and two police vehicles racing out of the station garage and knew they were only minutes away. I kept Jerri on the line until I confirmed the emergency crew was on the scene. I heard Beck's voice calling to someone in the background and experienced a sense of confidence. He would make sure everyone was okay.

I clicked off the call and finished entering everything necessary in the system, moving onto a data project Chief Masters had asked me to handle. My mind spun to Beck. I was utterly positive everyone would be fine solely because he was there. It was ridiculous how much confidence I had in him. The full crew from the firefighters to the police to the EMT's would be responsible for handling everything. If anything, Beck's crew might have less to do in this kind of emergency. They'd help deal with getting everyone safely out of the camper and manage whatever needed to be done to get the camper upright and off the road. The EMT's would do the heavy lifting as far as taking care of anyone injured.

But it was Beck, so he was the hero in my mind. I'd gone from hot fantasies about him to even hotter reality with him. I'd also gone from being close to hating him because he teased me so much to mentally swooning over him.

You're gaga over him now. It's so bad it's embarrassing.

So what? Since when did I decide I couldn't have any fun?

Since you had enough sense to know no man sticks around. You know the deal. Take care of yourself because no one else will.

That little voice trying to argue the last point stayed quiet after that. For as long as I could remember, I'd been almost solely in charge of taking care of myself. What happened in the three short years of my life before my mother died might have been different, but I certainly didn't remember.

My clear recollections, as early as when I was in kindergarten, all involved me picking up the slack for my father. I went to my first day of kindergarten without a lunch box. I'd never been to kindergarten, so my small child's mind had no idea I'd needed one. That night, I'd pleaded with my father to take me to the store and get one. He'd eventually sent me off with his girlfriend of the moment. I didn't even remember her name, but she'd seemed as befuddled by the task as he had. She'd taken me to the grocery store, which didn't have many choices, where I'd selected a bright blue plastic lunch box that went on to remain my lunch box all the way through fourth grade. Heavy duty plastic was amazing stuff. Thank goodness because it wasn't likely my father would've thought ahead to get me another lunch box.

It wasn't that I hadn't dated at all, although I wasn't even sure that's what I'd say I was doing with Beck. I'd had a sort of boyfriend in high school and then a few more sort of boyfriends in college. Nothing really clicked. I was always too serious. I'd never quite figured out the carefree, fun attitude. Anyway, my point was I'd liked guys before but I'd *never, ever* started thinking about them in terms of how safe they made me feel. Beck had morphed into this hazy hero in my mind. He could take care of anyone and everyone. Including me.

I didn't need anyone to take care of me though. I was in charge of me and always would be. It was risky and silly to count on anyone else. Yet, here I was, somehow thinking I could relax and count on Beck to be there for me.

I was in the middle of shaking my head firmly back and forth—in response to my own stupid internal dialogue—when Amelia pushed through the door to the station.

Amelia was gorgeous. She was tall, as tall as most men. Leggy, with generous curves and amber hair and eyes, it didn't surprise me in the least that Cade was so ridiculously in love with her. I didn't know their entire story, but they were one of those meant-to-be couples, or so I'd heard, after they'd been hot and heavy in high school and college. Rumor had it they had a messy break up, and Cade left town. When he came back, I occasionally wondered if he might burst into flames when she was around. Smoldering was apt when it came to the way he looked at her.

She stopped and angled her head to the side, her gaze quizzical. "That bad to see me?"

"Oh no. I wasn't shaking my head at you, just, uh, something else," I said, rather lamely.

I wasn't about to share I'd been obsessing over Beck and how ridiculous I felt about him.

Amelia smiled and came to lean her elbows on the counter surrounding me. "So, you'll be there tonight?" she asked.

She must've caught the confusion on my face.

"Our girls' card night," she clarified.

"Oh right. I forgot all about it."

I had absolutely no plans. Because I rarely ever had plans. Yet, for a beat, I hesitated. What if Beck wanted to come over again?

You have no idea what Beck wants to do. You could use a few friends for the first time in your life, so just go.

Well, geez. That side of me could be a tad bossy. The truth was, I wouldn't mind figuring out the friend thing. I wasn't going anywhere. As far as I could see into the future, I planned to stay right here in Willow Brook. I was far enough away from the freewheeling life of my father, I could mostly count on him not showing up and asking to borrow money as he'd been prone to do when I lived nearby. I had a good job, a house, a truck and everything else Gram left me. I also had more stability than I'd ever had. If there was one thing I craved, it was that.

I met Amelia's gaze and nodded. "I'll be there. I don't think I ever got the deets on when and where."

"Lucy's place. She lives above our office just down the street. Do you know where I mean?"

"How could I miss that sign?" I said with a laugh, referring to her Kick A** Construction company sign in bright blue.

Amelia flashed a grin. "Right. I did think of that when I named it. I hoped it would mean people would remember who I was."

"Considering how busy Cade says you are, I'd say you have."

"Speaking of Cade, is he around or out on a call?"

Beck's team was officially on duty for local calls today, but that didn't mean Cade hadn't tagged along. I tapped the intercom button on my headset. "Cade, you around?" I asked at large, knowing my question would be heard throughout the station.

"Headed your way, Maisie," Cade returned.

Within seconds, Cade pushed through the door. Amelia spun toward him, her face lighting up. He tugged her flush against him and kissed her. The moment was quick, but so hot, I had to look away. It was usually like this between them. Beck had dubbed Cade *Amelia-blind* because of the way he lost track of everything else when she was around. It blew me away if only because they'd known each other forever.

I kept my focus on the tracking sheet I'd been working on and entered a few more numbers, glancing up only when I heard my name.

"Huh?"

Cade winked. "I hear you're joining the girls' card game. Be careful. Lucy kicks ass at cards."

Amelia nudged him with her knee as she rested her elbows on the counter again. Her cheeks were flushed and her eyes bright. I experienced a pang of...something. I wouldn't call it envy because it wasn't that, more wistfulness. Watching Amelia and Cade together made me think about what it might be like to have something like they did. The intimacy between them was palpable. Underneath it was a feeling of shared joy and the sense they faced everything in life together. Amelia struck me as a very independent woman, while Cade was without a doubt a strong, independent man. They served to reinforce each other and clearly adored each other beyond reason.

Amelia caught my eyes. "Lucy *is* good, but we don't play for money, just fun."

"Just be prepared to lose," Cade added.

I had a streak of competitiveness when it came to cards, if only because I'd learned to play young. My father held weekly poker games no matter what else had been going on in our lives. Cards were the one area where he hewed to a sense of honor. He played clean and shared his sense of pride in winning with me. I had few fond memories with my dad and his haphazard parenting approach, but playing cards with him was one of them. He was quite good. As such, so was I.

"Consider me warned," I said with a grin.

Amelia pushed away from the counter

and hooked her arm with Cade's. "Lunch with me?"

"Of course," he replied easily.

I watched as they walked out, recalling how bitter Cade had been when he'd first moved back to Willow Brook. I'd been pretty new in my position then and hadn't known much of anything about anyone. He'd been a bit of a dark cloud around the station until he worked things out with Amelia.

Everything about him softened when she was around.

Chapter Twenty

BECK

"Dude, don't make me go alone," Cade said.

I eyed him across the table. We'd stopped by Wildlands after work. Cade had been at loose ends because Amelia was with her friends.

"You can handle it, man."

Cade shook his head, his gaze bordering on pleading. "Come on. It's Amelia, Lucy, Maisie and a few others. What is it with you anyway? Last month or so, you haven't even looked at a woman."

He idly twirled his empty beer bottle on the table, his perceptive gaze on me. I shifted my shoulders, slightly uncomfortable under his gaze. Cade knew me well. We'd grown up together. We'd grown apart when he moved away for seven years, but we'd quickly fallen back into a comfortable friendship when he returned. I respected the hell out of him and had complete trust in him out in the field. He knew his shit and had anyone's back when we were in deep with fire all around.

I hadn't considered the fact my patterns had changed. Quite a lot. Until this thing with Maisie started, I was usually at the bars, having a little light fun with any woman who caught my fancy. Now, even the thought of being with someone other than Maisie almost made me shudder. I glanced around the bar, my eyes passing over plenty of attractive women. Summers in Willow Brook drew plenty of women looking for an adventure with any rugged, Alaskan guy. Easy come, easy go. Usually, I loved it. The last few weeks I'd found it rather annoying to swat aside the come ons.

My gaze made its way back to Cade, and I shrugged. "So what?"

He narrowed his eyes and appeared to be considering his words. "Right. None of my business, but anything up with you and Maisie?"

Oh hell. Was I really going to have to dance around this?

"Nah," I lied. "Why do you ask?"

"Mostly because you two are usually arguing, but lately you seem to be avoiding her a lot more."

I couldn't exactly tell him that was the only way I could keep from trying to bend her over and fuck her anywhere I crossed her path. I knew she was sensitive to how it might be perceived if the guys knew we had anything going on, so I'd been steering mostly clear of her around the station.

I met Cade's gaze and shrugged. "No reason, just random I suppose. Anyway, let's get going."

Though I sensed he knew I was distracting him, Cade readily acceded. We left cash on the table to cover our tab and headed out into the late evening.

I knew it probably wasn't wise to tromp over to Lucy's gathering with him, knowing Maisie was there. But I couldn't resist. Any chance to see her was impossible to resist.

Spending the night with her the other night had only strengthened the foothold she had in my mind and body. I wasn't quite ready to admit my heart was involved, but I was damn certain it was.

———

Maisie sat at the kitchen table in Lucy Caldwell's apartment, laughing at something. Her ponytail was losing its battle to keep her curls restrained with many dark curls loose and dangling around her neck and face. One look, and I wanted to kiss her. She, however, hadn't even noticed I'd walked in. Amelia, Lucy, and Susannah circled the rest of the table.

Amelia was the first to notice we were there. She looked our way and grinned. "Lucy lost!" she announced.

Cade chuckled and stepped to the table to drop a kiss on the side of Amelia's neck.

Lucy rolled her eyes. "I didn't realize how excited you'd get over me losing."

Amelia giggled. She was quite obviously tipsy, which was why Cade was there. He'd become the designated driver once he got her text.

"It's just fun to have someone else win. That's all." She swung to look at Maisie. "You have an amazing poker face."

Maisie shrugged. "I guess so."

Her cheeks were flushed, and my cock was hard. Damn. I leaned my hips against the kitchen counter, hoping the slight angle would mask my blatant arousal. Coming here was a mistake.

Lucy stood up from the table. "Well boys, are you both here to play taxi?"

Cade leaned against the counter beside me and nodded. "Amelia texted me for a ride home. Who else needs a ride?"

Maisie finally appeared to notice me, her eyes widening and the flush on her cheeks deepening. The effect of nothing more than a look from her wasn't helping matters with my cock.

"Well, since there's two of you here, I say you take me and Susannah, and Beck can take Maisie. Susannah's place is on our way home. Maisie lives in the opposite direction," Amelia announced with a slight giggle.

Cade glanced to me, his gaze bemused, before looking back to her. "What's so funny, babe?"

Amelia shrugged and giggled again.

Cade shook his head. "Good thing you've got me to drive you."

Maisie swung to look at Amelia. "I don't need a ride," she said, her tone slightly belligerent.

Susannah piped up. "Yes, you do. We've had two bottles of wine between the four of us."

Even Susannah's words slurred slightly.

I wasn't about to argue with being offered

up as Maisie's ride, so I stayed quiet. Not to mention I wasn't about to allow her to drive home in her current state. I wouldn't let any friend drive home like this, but she drew my protectiveness to the fore so forcefully, it was startling.

Maisie huffed. "I can drive just fine."

At that moment, she leaned back in her chair, a tad too forcefully, and promptly toppled sideways. I didn't even think and was beside her, helping her back into her chair, before I knew it.

"You just proved my point," Susannah declared with a floppy wave of her hand.

I glanced around the table. This was quite the sight. Lucy plunked back down in her chair with an elaborate sigh. Every single one of them had flushed cheeks and a slightly hazy gaze.

"Amelia's right. No one's driving home," I said, catching Cade's eyes.

Who knew their girls' card night meant they'd all get sloshed?

Cade chuckled. "Definitely not. You two ready?" he asked, glancing from Amelia to Susannah.

When they both gave wobbly nods, I glanced down to Maisie. My hand was resting on her shoulder from when I'd helped her back into her chair. That single point of contact set my body to humming. Hell, I'd been hard since I'd laid eyes on her, but touching her just made things worse.

"Sounds like I'm your taxi."

She lifted her gaze, her liquid brown eyes locking with mine. Something flickered in their depths, but I didn't know what it was. "I think I can..."

I shook my head. "You're not driving anywhere. Either you let me take you home, or you stay here. Lucy, you want company?" I asked, looking to her.

Lucy sent a pointed glare in Maisie's direction. "Don't be silly. I don't mind if you crash on my couch, but lover boy's right here to take you home."

Oh hell. I had no idea where that comment came from.

I glanced back to Maisie to see her cheeks had gone cherry red. Amelia and Susannah were standing up from the table and appeared to have missed Lucy's comment. Cade, on the other hand, caught my eyes and threw a knowing grin my way.

I ignored him and looked back to Maisie. "Well, what'll it be? A ride with me, or a night on Lucy's couch?"

Maisie didn't reply, but she stood, wobbling slightly on her feet when she did. Without thinking, I slid my arm around her waist to steady her.

"Good choice," Lucy declared with an overenthusiastic nod.

Within moments, we'd managed to say our goodbyes without further comment, and I was helping Maisie into my truck. She lost her balance when her foot slipped off of the running board. When I caught her weight against me—fuck, she felt good, all soft and warm—she muttered something.

"What was that?" I asked.

"I don't need your help," she said with a firm elbow in the direction of my ribs. Her aim was off, and she ended up slamming her elbow against the side of the truck.

"Ow!"

"You okay?"

"Yeah, but that hurt," she said, now attempting to rub her elbow with her other hand.

I'd been trying to let her get herself in the truck and mostly standing by for back up. Now, I took over and lifted her against me, setting her on the passenger seat.

"I told you..."

I cut in. "I know. You don't need my help. Clearly you do. If I hadn't been here, you'd be on the ground at this point. It's a damn good thing your friends weren't about to let you drive yourself home."

She had nothing to say to that, so I buckled her seat belt and closed the door. She was quiet as I started driving toward her place, so I stayed quiet as well. My cock was still hard. Having an armful of Maisie was pretty much a guaranteed way for me to end up burning up with need for her. I mentally willed it away because I knew there'd be no relief tonight. I might want her so bad, I physically ached with it, but she was too drunk.

We pulled into her driveway, and I made the quick choice not to ask her if she needed help getting inside. She was quiet and surprised me by not arguing a bit when I walked to her door with her. I followed her inside, closing the door behind me. I might be setting myself up for a hell of a tortuous night, but I didn't want to leave. I wanted to fall asleep beside her again.

She startled me by spinning around and catching the edge of my t-shirt and yanking me to her. Next thing I knew, her lips were blazing a hot, wet trail up my neck. It took just about every ounce of willpower I had to draw back and set her away from me.

"Bed for you," I said quickly, turning and catching her hand as I did.

"You're bossy," she announced as we were halfway up the stairs.

The toe of her shoe caught the edge of the top stair, and she stumbled slightly. I steadied her at the hips. She spun around, wobbling again. I tightened my hold to keep her from falling.

I was one step below her, so we were about level. Her eyes locked to me. In a flash, the air felt weighted. She looped her arms around my neck and stepped closer, bumping against my rock hard cock.

Much as I wanted her, and holy hell did I want her, this wasn't happening. Not tonight. Not with her so tipsy she could hardly stand. I slid my hands down her sides, savoring the soft swell of her breasts as I passed by them and gripped her hips, setting her back.

I turned her and quickly stepped past her, latching onto her hand and walking her into her bedroom.

She plunked down on the end of the bed, bouncing slightly. She giggled. Maisie *giggled*. My heart clenched, and I felt funny inside. I gulped in air and stared down at her, willing my heart to stop pounding so hard it hurt.

I meant to say something, but then

Maisie simply curled up on her side and was out inside of two seconds. I watched her for a moment. Without thinking, I reached down and brushed a few loose curls off of her cheek. My heart gave another swift kick, this one hard enough to maybe crack a rib.

I straightened, considering whether I should stay or go. The answer came easy. I had to stay. I couldn't force myself to leave. With another glance to confirm she was sound asleep—snoring and all—I walked quietly out of her room and went downstairs to make sure everything was locked up.

After returning to her bedroom, I carefully got her jeans off and even managed to unhook her bra and maneuver it out of her t-shirt. Her panties had gotten tangled in her jeans, sending a jolt of need through me. Getting them back on was more work, so I left them off and gave myself a stern lecture about letting her sleep. She was so sound asleep, she didn't even awaken when I lifted her from the bottom of the bed and tucked her in under the covers. Once I was sure she was comfortable, I took an icy cold shower.

A few minutes later, I managed to slide under the sheets without waking her. As soon as I settled onto my back, she rolled over, hooked her leg over mine and tucked her head against my shoulder, her palm landing smack in the middle of my chest. I'd never thought much about the sleeping together part when it came to women. One night with Maisie had made me crave more of it with her. I stared up through the skylight above her bed, feeling the day's tension inside unwind and savoring the soft warmth of her curled up against me.

Chapter Twenty-One

MAISIE

I burrowed closer to the warm, strong body beside me. Oh God. It felt sooo good to...

My sleepy thoughts faded slightly, and for a moment I was confused. The haze cleared, and I realized the body beside me belonged to Beck. I was practically on top of him. The moment my brain was fully online, I realized I was slick with desire, and his cock was plenty hard, pressed against my hip.

Oh.

Well then.

My recollections of last night were fuzzy. I'd definitely had a bit too much wine. The last memory I had was walking up the stairs with Beck and thinking I wanted to have him buried deep inside of me. Everything was blank after that. I conducted a quick inventory. I was wearing no panties and a t-shirt. Hmm.

I rose up on one elbow and looked at him. Damn. He was even drool-worthy when he was asleep. His black curls were mussed. In sleep, his face was more relaxed. I let myself soak him in for a minute. For so long, I'd had to truncate my desire to stare at him. His features were what I thought would be called *chiseled*. His jaw was strong and defined, and damn if he didn't have actual sculpted cheekbones, the kind most women would die for. His nose was a clean straight line. His dark, thick lashes curled against his cheeks. His mouth was made for sin—full lips with a slight dimple in the center of the bottom one.

Before I realized what I was doing, I'd leaned over and kissed Beck. Because his lips were that tempting. His lips came alive under mine. We tumbled into a slow, lazy kiss—a sensual tangle of tongues. He was an insanely good kisser—dangerously good. It was ridiculous how easily he could melt me. Once his tongue swept into my mouth, it felt as if molten lava flowed through me. His palm slid around to cup my bottom and shift me on top of him.

My knees landed alongside his hips with my wet pussy sliding over his cock. I moaned into his mouth, so on fire inside I could barely breathe. I broke free from our kiss to gulp in air. I felt his hand slide into my hair, his thumb tracing my lips. Opening my eyes, I found his waiting—deep green and flashing with desire.

"Morning," he murmured, his voice gravelly with sleep.

All it took was the sound of his voice to send a shiver up my spine. Looking into his eyes, my heart twisted in my chest and my breath caught. All this time, I'd chalked him up to a shallow playboy. Perhaps he was, but it didn't feel that way when I was with him.

Desire and intimacy curled around us like smoke. I couldn't have looked away if I wanted to. I didn't.

"Good morning," I whispered.

It was early, or so the wispy light filtering in through my curtains and the skylight above told me. It felt as if we were the only people in the entire world awake just now.

He traced my lips with his thumb. I caught it in my teeth and drew it in my mouth, feeling a surge of desire when his eyes darkened and he rocked his hips against me. His cock slid against my slick folds and clit, sending a sharp spike of pleasure through me. I leaned back, the need to feel him inside of me overriding everything.

Reaching between us, I rose up and was a millisecond away from sinking down when his hands gripped my hips roughly. I whipped my head up to look at him.

His gaze was fierce, searing me straight through to my heart.

"Don't rush this," he said roughly.

I swallowed against the sudden tightness in my throat and held still for a beat. The head of his cock kissed the entrance of my pussy—I ached to feel him fill me. On the heels of a breath, I adjusted my hips and slid slowly down, savoring the delicious stretch of him filling me to the hilt.

I stilled once I was seated. "Was that slow enough?" I asked, my voice husked with need.

His hands eased their grip on my hips and slid down to rest at the juncture of my thighs, his thumbs brushing softly across the hypersensitive skin there. I could hardly breathe—swamped in need with emotion coursing through me.

I forced myself to hold still. I was caught between impulses. There was the raw physical need to seek relief by losing myself in this. Yet, there was also the need to stay with him in this, to listen. Not listening in the specific sense of responding to what he said, more listening on a visceral level.

"It was," he said, that gruff voice sending a ripple straight through me.

He began to rock into me, easing my hips in time with his motion. We fell into a slow, sensuous rhythm. His eyes stayed locked to mine, and I couldn't look away. Pleasure shot through me again and again and again with every rock of his hips into mine. Pressure tightened inside until I was chasing after the hot, sweet release I knew was coming. My breath came in messy pants and moans.

His palm slid up my back in a slow pass, angling me forward, creating just enough pressure against my clit the next time he sank inside of me. I heard myself crying out his name as the pressure spun so tight it hurt and then unraveled with a snap, sending pleasure shooting through me.

He went taut underneath me, a rough cry escaping. He caught me fast as I collapsed atop him. I lay still against him, gasping to catch my breath. I could feel his heart pounding against me, echoing the wild beat of mine. I slowly relaxed, sweet lassitude sliding through me.

Chapter Twenty-Two

BECK

Maisie was a tangle of softness and silky skin against me. Buried deep inside of her, I didn't want to move. Ever. I sifted my fingers through her curls. She started to shift her weight off of me, but I held her tight.

"Don't move," I murmured.

She laughed softly. "You're bossy this morning."

She lifted her head, her brown eyes glinting with mirth.

"Am I?"

She nodded, her messy curls bouncing. "Don't rush, don't move. What else shouldn't I do?"

Her comment reminded me I'd told her not to rush somewhere along the way of that hot little interlude we'd just experienced. My heart tightened for a beat, and I had to take a slow breath to gather myself. She had the craziest effect on me. I hadn't wanted any of this to end too soon. Hell, if we could've somehow made these moments last forever, I would've.

I didn't know what to do with any of these feelings, so I shrugged and grinned. It was pretty much impossible not to smile when she was. "No more orders."

Her stomach growled. She promptly put her hand over it. "Oh my God. That was loud."

"How about you move now? We can shower, and I'll make breakfast."

I couldn't quite believe I'd just said that. But I had. I was pretty set in my ways with women. I rarely spent the night. If I did, I was up and gone before dawn. I didn't plan on showers and lazy mornings with breakfast, but that's all I wanted with Maisie.

Her grin faded as she looked at me. After a moment when my heart started banging madly against my ribs again, she angled her head to the side.

"You cook?"

"I do. Quite well, actually."

Her wide grin made me want to hug her.

Maisie was the one and only person in the world who elicited that urge in me. Just now, I made do with sliding my hand in a slow pass down her spine. My cock twitched. I could take her all over again right now, only minutes after spending myself inside of her.

"My mom loved to cook, so she used to have me in the kitchen with her all the time when I was little. Turns out, that's an easy way to learn to cook," I added by way of explanation.

"Oh," Maisie said softly.

I sensed something shifting under the waters of our conversation, but I didn't know what it was. "My mom passed away a few years ago. I miss her like crazy, but I think of her whenever I cook."

My words just slipped out...and startled the hell out of me. I wasn't prone to sharing like this with anyone. It was true I missed my mom. My dad was still around and had been at loose ends ever since she died. He'd pieced together a life that worked for him, but he missed her. I'd been lucky that way. I had two parents who'd loved me all through my childhood.

Maisie held my gaze and nodded slowly. "I'm sorry she's gone."

"Me too. But it's life, right? I was lucky

she was around as long as she was. She was diagnosed with breast cancer when I was little. Lucked out and kicked it to the curb, but it came back later."

Maisie seemed pensive, and I wasn't quite sure what to make of it. Hell, I was enough off kilter with my own unexpectedly personal comments. She nodded again and shifted her weight, slowly rising off of me. I resisted the urge to hold her in place and followed her into the shower.

In short order, we were downstairs. She started coffee, while I rummaged in her refrigerator to see what I could whip up for breakfast.

"Mind if I use these eggs and some cheese?" I said, glancing over my shoulder.

"Use whatever you want."

I quickly prepped omelets. She watched with a half grin and handed me a fresh cup of coffee somewhere along the way. It was the kind of morning I hadn't had in years. Well, I'd never had a morning like this, not with a woman I supposed I was dating. Or something more. It was the kind of morning my parents had—relaxed and sharing space together. I'd lived alone ever since I'd moved out of my parents' place. I was a fairly typical bachelor with the exception I ate pretty well for myself. It was more fun to cook for someone else though.

Maisie was putting our empty plates in the dishwasher a while later when there was a loud knock at the door. She looked to me. "Are you expecting anyone?"

"Me? It's your house," I replied with a chuckle.

"Yeah, but no one comes to see me," she said, looking perplexed.

She stepped to the door and opened it. I was seated at the kitchen counter, finishing my cup of coffee, a rather delicious cup of coffee I might add. I had a direct view of the door.

She went still, so still I could see it from where I sat. Her spine stiffened, and I heard the sharp intake of her breath. A man stood there. He was tall and lanky with almost white hair. His face was weathered. I couldn't say why, but I was instantly protective of Maisie.

I set my coffee down just as she spoke.

"Dad, what are you doing here?" she asked, her tone startled.

"Maisie, girl! I'm here to see you, why else would I be here?"

He pulled her into a hug, and I could see her tense up. The man I now knew to be her father spoke in a jovial manner. He stepped through the door, although she hadn't invited him in.

My mind rifled through the bits of information I knew of Maisie's childhood from Carol. Carol had been the admin assistant at the station for many years. Her husband had passed away years before she did. I knew they'd had one daughter who'd moved away after falling in love with some guy who'd been hiking in Alaska one summer. I knew Carol had been devastated when her daughter died. I'd never heard a single negative word from her about Maisie's father, yet I'd surmised he wasn't too stable.

I watched as he stepped into the kitchen and looked around. His gaze glanced off of me. Maisie closed the door behind him. She didn't look at me. She stayed right where she was by the door, tension and a sense of weariness emanating from her. Her father took in the space—it was a lovely home. Carol had renovated the entire home only a few years before she passed away. Bright and airy, the space was inviting.

Maisie's father's gaze rounded back to her. "Nice place you have here," he said with a nod before promptly walking into the living room and plunking down on the couch.

Beyond the curved kitchen counter was the living room. With windows extending up two stories to the ceiling, there was no need for any lighting during the day. Even at this early-ish hour in the morning, it was bright. There was a sectional couch at an angle in the center of the room, offering a view out the windows from one side and facing the flat-screen television mounted on the wall from the other. I'd actually helped Carol put that up after my mother asked me to help. Aside from the couch, there was a large, cushioned ottoman and a few tables scattered about the room.

Maisie finally moved, walking past me, her eyes flicking to me briefly. Her gaze was stony and controlled, reminiscent of the look she used to have so often back when she first showed up at the station to fill in after her grandmother passed away. She stopped at the corner of the couch, resting a hand on her hip.

"Dad, what are you doing here?" she asked, her tone low with only a hint of the frustration I sensed coming off of her in waves.

Uncertain if she wanted my support, I stood and walked to her side. I didn't know who her father was to her, but I knew without a doubt she was upset at his abrupt appearance.

He glanced up from the couch. "Gonna introduce me to your boyfriend?" he asked, completely ignoring her actual question.

"Dad, he's..."

I cut in, sliding my arm around her shoulders as I did. "I'm Beck. Beck Steele," I said with a firm nod. "Mind answering Maisie's question?"

Her father, whose name I still didn't know, eyed me for a beat. His white hair was unkempt and messy, his eyes a light gray. He looked a little worse for the wear, but gave off a sense of entitlement. "Hank Thomas," he finally said with a nod. He looked from me to Maisie and shrugged. "Just thought I'd come up for a visit."

I could feel the tension thrumming in her body. I wanted to demand he leave and then do whatever was necessary to get her to relax again. I didn't like seeing her like this. I slid my palm down her spine and back up. She relaxed into my side slightly, and I took a breath. I forced myself to stay quiet. I had so little information to piece together her reaction to him, and I didn't want to overstep my bounds. I was fairly certain she'd been about to dispute her father's description of me as her boyfriend, while I'd cemented his perception by cutting in like that. I didn't give a damn. In fact, I was more than happy for him to see me that way. Hell, I was ready to announce it to the world. I just had to wait and make certain Maisie was on board with it.

Her shoulders rose and fell with a deep breath, and I slid my palm in another pass along her spine. I didn't know what she meant to say to her father, but I was here for her however she needed me to be.

"Dad, since when do you visit? I moved out when I was eighteen and lived in California no more than a half hour away most of the time, and you hardly visited for seven years. When you did, it was because you needed money. You haven't called in the entire two years since I moved up here. What are you doing here?" she repeated, her voice cracking at the end.

My heart clenched at that little crack in her voice, revealing the fissure in her composure.

If Hank picked up on how distressed she was, he didn't let on. He merely shrugged. "What's wrong with your good old dad coming for a visit?"

Well, that comment went over well. Maisie's spine went ramrod straight. I glanced sideways to see her nostrils flare and two bright pink spots appear high on her cheekbones.

"Dad, you were never my good old dad. I don't know what you want from me, but drop the song and dance. What do you need? Money?"

I was taking little stabs in the dark to figure out the dynamics here, but so help me God, if her father was here to bully her into giving him money, hell no as far as I was concerned. I forced myself to stay quiet though. It wasn't yet time for me to force myself any further into the situation than I already had.

Hank's eyes narrowed at her comment. He seemed remarkably unsurprised by it. "You just can't believe I might want to visit. Damn, Maisie. After your mom died, I raised you all by myself. Give me some credit. I coulda sent you up here to stay with your Gram, but I tried to do right by you."

Okay, now I was furious. I might be short on the details, but one thing was becoming clear. Hank didn't give much of a damn about Maisie.

"Well, my life would've been a lot better if you had let me stay here," Maisie retorted. "Now just drop the bullshit. What do you need?"

"Alright fine. I wanted to visit for a few days, but it wouldn't hurt if you could help me out with some bills,' Hank said, his tone so *not* chastened, I wanted to punch him.

"How the hell did you swing a plane ticket if you need money?" I demanded, forgetting I was trying to let Maisie handle this.

"Got a deal from my girlfriend. She works in baggage claim at the airport," he said with a shrug.

If Maisie was upset with me jumping in, she didn't say anything. In fact, she'd gone quiet. Her shoulders were so tense under my arm, I was worried.

I glanced to her. Her features were tight and drawn, and she looked on the verge of tears. I wanted Hank the hell out of here and fast.

I realized the manners my mother had drilled into me weren't helping just now. I didn't need to stand here in front of this asshole just because. He wasn't a guest. I turned, and Maisie didn't hesitate, allowing me to lead her away. I aimed straight for the bathroom, seeing as it was that, or walk all the way upstairs for some privacy.

Once we were in there, I closed the door. Maisie leaned her back against the wall and buried her face in her hands. I waited, unsure what to do. After a moment, I heard her breath catch in a sob and finally gave into what I'd been wanting to do ever since her father showed up at the door. I pulled her into my arms and just held her. She tensed for a second and then relaxed against me, letting her hands fall from her face when she buried it against my chest.

After several shuddering breaths while my heart clenched at the knowledge she was crying and so hurt by her father, she slipped her arms around my waist and gulped in air.

"My dad's a loser," she mumbled against my chest. "I'm sorry he showed up like this."

I sifted my fingers through her hair, torn between a visceral ache at seeing her upset like this and anger with her father for putting her in this situation. "What are you apologizing for? He's the one who showed up out of the blue. For the record, I couldn't give a shit about your dad, or whether he's a loser or not. I just don't like seeing you like this. If you want me to throw him out for you, I will. Just tell me what you need."

She lifted her head, her wide brown eyes so unguarded, it was like a punch to my gut. "I don't know. I'm used to dealing with everything myself. I mean, he's my dad. I'll just give him some money and he'll go away."

I bit back the curses I wanted to rain down on his head. "Is that what you want to do?"

She bit her lip, her mouth twisting and a sad look entering her eyes. "No, but it will make him go away. Look, he's not a bad guy, he's just a mess. He can't be bothered for much of anything."

I had all kinds of things I wanted to say, most of them involving trashing her dad and escorting him out of her life because I hated seeing the pain and weariness he brought into her eyes. I beat back those words and took a breath.

"Okay, if you don't want to give him money, don't give him money. If I pieced together a few things right, he's hit you up before. Every time you say yes, it will set him up to come back next time he wants more. How about this? I'll call in a favor from a buddy of mine in Anchorage. I can probably get him a night at the hotel there. I'll buy him a one-way ticket back to wherever he came from. He doesn't need to know anything about who takes care of his ticket."

Maisie stared at me, worrying her bottom lip. "I don't know. I can't ask you to do that. I mean, I have to deal with this. It's not..."

"You *don't* have to deal with this alone." My words came out fiercer than I intended.

She was quiet and then suddenly her eyes glistened and a tear rolled down her cheek. Oh fuck. My heart clenched again. I brushed her tear away with my thumb.

To say I was stumbling along through this was a massive understatement. I had no fucking clue what I was doing. My single goal was to make Maisie feel better. Now, she was crying, and I didn't know quite why.

"Look, we can do whatever you want. I was just offering that to..."

She dragged her sleeve across her cheeks and nose, shaking her head.

"It's okay. I feel like shit. I mean, he's my dad. I just hate how he pulls this crap."

"I bet."

She sniffled and scrubbed at her cheeks again. I reached to the side and snagged a tissue out of the box on the bathroom counter.

As soon as I handed it to her, she blew her nose noisily in it and tossed the tissue in the trash. On the heels of a shuddering breath, she looked back up at me. "I don't feel right shoving him out the door to Anchorage. I'll call Janet and see if she can find a spot for him at her B&B."

"Still want me to book him a ticket?"

It killed me to step back and let her make this call, but I knew I had to. Even if he was a loser, he was her dad.

She shrugged. "I'm not sure yet. If you do, I'll pay you back."

I shook my head, only to have her shake hers back emphatically. Her curls, still damp from our shower, swung back and forth.

I chuckled. When she grinned a little, relief hit me. I hated, fucking hated, seeing her upset. It might be only a brief respite, but seeing that small smile made me want to shout.

That's how deeply Maisie had burrowed into my heart. Damn.

I didn't have time to ponder this, so I forced my focus to the moment. "We can argue about that later. You sure? Because if you say so, as soon as we get him outta here, I'll make those reservations."

"It's never good for me to have him around too long, but let me talk to him before you make the reservations."

She took another deep breath and stepped back. I instantly missed her warmth and softness against me. I wanted to keep her held close, to protect her from anything that might hurt her. I shackled the urge to pull her back to me. For one, she looked ready to go back out and face her dad. For another, he was out there waiting and wouldn't be going anywhere until we dealt with him.

So I let my hands fall reluctantly. She looked over at me. "Do I look like I was just crying?"

Her cheeks were a little pink, and her eyes barely damp. My heart thumped. Hard.

"Doesn't matter if you do, but not really. Tell me what the plan is before I go out there and make an ass of myself."

Chapter Twenty-Three

MAISIE

Later that afternoon, I finished a call and spun around to take care of some filing. I had my head halfway in the filing cabinet when I heard my name.

"Hang on," I mumbled, rolling my chair back.

The top of my ponytail caught on the filing cabinet as I straightened up. I grabbed my hair with one hand and spun around. "Can I help you?" I asked automatically as I wrestled my now loose curls back into submission.

I glanced up to find Janet laughing.

"Oh hey. Did you need something official?"

She leaned an elbow on the counter and

shook her head. "Nope. Rumor has it you might need me to scrounge up a room."

"Do you have anything open? I know it's last minute, but..."

She waved me quiet. "I usually keep one room open, so it's yours on one condition."

I snapped the elastic around my ponytail and looked over at her, instantly suspicious. "Um, okay. What?"

Her brown eyes crinkled at the corners with her grin. "Tell me what's going on with you and Beck."

My cheeks got hot. I mentally berated myself. I should've immediately connected the dots. The only person who knew I was scouting for a room for my dad was Beck. Beck had gone above and beyond this morning, and I was wrestling with how I felt about it. Between being an absolute rock when I pretty much fell apart this morning, he'd volunteered to take my dad and drop him off with Chief Masters for some firefighter and police joint training event. He'd figured it was the safest way to keep my dad occupied and out of my hair all day. Seeing as my dad had hitchhiked to my house from Anchorage, he didn't have much say in the matter. Beck had firmly escorted him out and backed me up completely on my dad not staying with me for a few days.

I wasn't used to having anyone to lean on. I didn't quite know what to think of it. Layering this on top of the rest of my muddled feelings about Beck only added to my inner confusion. The strangest part was it felt good, so good I almost pinched myself. Every time that feeling passed through me, it was like emotional whiplash. I couldn't trust it, so I got annoyed and angry with myself.

Janet cleared her throat. Oh, right. She was waiting while I sat here mooning about Beck all in my own head. I looked back into her kind brown eyes and shrugged.

"What do you mean?"

I tried to sound innocent, but Janet wasn't having it. She cocked her head to one side and arched a brow.

"Let me see. Well, apparently Beck was at your house at the crack of dawn. He also appears to be your father's taxi for the day. He delivered your dad to the police chief and stopped by the café to give me a heads up you'd be asking about a room for your dad. He didn't give much away, but I'm no dummy."

My cheeks were so hot at this point, I needed to splash water on my face to cool off.

Seeing as that wasn't an option right this second, I steeled myself and met Janet's way too perceptive gaze.

"We might be seeing each other. Please don't say anything. I don't want the other guys here to be weird. This job is really important to me and..."

Janet's gaze softened. "Hey, you know I'd never talk. I might know everything because, well, my café's as close to the center of the universe as you can find in Willow Brook, but I don't gossip myself. Not about anything important. Far as I'm concerned, I'm beyond thrilled to see you step out of your comfort zone. You've been like a turtle here, keeping to yourself too much. Plus, I happen to think Beck's a good guy. He sure seems to think you're special."

I stared at her, uncertain for a moment how to respond. Janet simply looked back at me, arching her brow. The warmth in her gaze helped ease the tension bundled inside my chest.

I sighed. "Okay fine. We might be seeing each other. I just don't want anybody else to know about it. I don't know what the other guys would think around the station."

Janet shrugged. "I'm not the other guys, hon. I get why you might want to keep it quiet. But don't try to convince yourself you 'might' be seeing Beck. Far as I can tell, he's damn serious about you. He's lugging your dad around and making sure he has a place to say. Speaking of your dad, what the hell is he doing here?"

Emotion tightened in my chest and a familiar sad, weary feeling rose inside. That's how I always felt when I thought about my dad. He was my dad, the only one I had, and I loved him, but I wished he could stop the endless merry-go-round of his chaotic life. I wished he wasn't visiting only because he needed money. I knew he didn't see it that way. I doubted he ever thought much about how his actions might be perceived by me, or anyone else for that matter. He wasn't that deep. He was charismatic and fun and drew people into his orbit easily. The mundane, less exciting parts of life, such as paying bills, were an afterthought to him. Hence, he turned wherever he could when he found himself too far into a bad spot financially.

"He needs money, and he flew all the way to Alaska to get it," I said flatly. "Sounds like he got some deal for his plane ticket from his girlfriend. She probably got it for him. I don't know what to do. Beck says I shouldn't give him any money because every time I do, he'll just come back for more."

"Beck's damn straight on that," Janet said, her eyes snapping. Her lips tightened into a thin line. "Don't let him do this to you. You don't deserve it. I know he's your dad but..."

I cut in. "Exactly. That's the problem. He's my dad—the only one I've got. I know he's a loser. I know it's not good that he pulls this shit, but I can't just say no."

My heart ached a little, and I felt small inside. I'd spent so much of my life jumping up and down and waving my arms for my dad's attention. Just the attention to get my basic needs met. He pulled on the worn strings of my heart no matter what he did.

Janet's eyes softened again. "Hon, you can love your dad, but you can say no to this. He's not starving. He probably just needs a little to get by. Don't let him mooch off of you. He needs to stop hurting you like this. Beck's right. He'll just keep coming back." She paused, angling her head to the side. "How many times has he done this?"

I shrugged. "I don't know. Probably once a year or so ever since I moved out. Well, except since I moved up here. This is the first time he's shown up here."

"Hon, I can't tell you what to do, but I'm

gonna anyway. Your dad might not be a bad guy, but he's always been the one to look for the easy way out, no matter whose back he climbs over. This is just what he does, and as long as you let him do it, he'll keep doing it. If you want to have any chance to have a halfway decent relationship with him, at least step back. He's a charming ne'er-do-well and always was. That's how he swept your mom off her feet. She fell in love and lust with him just long enough to end up in a real bad spot. If Beck had his way, he'd already be driving your dad to Anchorage and putting him on a plane. I got a room for your dad. How about this? He stays for tonight, long enough for you to have a short and sweet visit. Make sure he understands you're not gonna keep giving him money whenever he asks. You're not his personal bank. Tomorrow, let Beck drive him to Anchorage to take that plane. Sound like a plan?"

I stared at her. Guilt crept into my thoughts. It was so hard to set a limit with my dad. Even though I knew he'd only been halfway there for me my entire childhood, it could've been so much worse and I knew it. In the only way he knew how to be a dad, he had tried. It had been a half-assed effort, but that was about all he could do. I knew Janet was right.

I took a deep breath, trying to will away my guilt and soothe my anxiety, and nodded. "Okay, I'll try. Do you need me to pay you for his room because I know he doesn't have the money?"

She shook her head slowly. "No, hon. Don't worry about it. How about you plan to stop by the café after your shift here? We can grab a bite together. No matter what I think of your dad because everything that went down with your mom, I'd rather be with you when you need to deal with him. Okay?"

My chest felt full. Between Janet and Beck, I wasn't used to having help like this. I was used to facing everything on my own. It was such a relief to know that I had people like this making sure I wasn't handling everything by myself. Yet, it was an odd feeling, something I wasn't accustomed to. Emotion welled inside again. I breathed through it.

"Deal," I said.

Janet stepped back from the counter and flashed a grin. "So, if Beck wants to join us, will that be okay?"

I stared at her. I knew perfectly well that he likely would and that meant us doing something publicly. My mind spun as I contemplated the implications of that. As if she could predict the direction I was going inside my head, Janet eyed me.

"Don't make it a thing. You're friends with all the guys that you work with here. Any one of them would grab an after work coffee at my place with you. If you make it more than it is, then everything will seem obvious. It's obvious you need to take some time to sort out what's going on with you two, but don't be all cloak and dagger. Trust me if you want to make gossip spread like a brushfire, that's the fastest way to do it."

At that, she winked, spun around and left. I sat at my desk staring out the front windows and then gave myself a little shake. I got back to filing, my mind jumping rope between what to do about my dad and what to do about Beck.

Chapter Twenty-Four

BECK

I walked beside Cade, tugging my heavy-duty fire gloves off and slapping them against my legs, knocking the dirt loose. He did the same as we walked. I paused for a moment and turned back to look at the flames shooting into the sky behind us. Today was one of several annual exercises that we conducted with the EMT's, the police and the firefighters. We'd set up out at the town's transfer station and essentially lit a bunch of garbage on fire. My crew and Cade's had finished our rotation. The last crew was stepping in to handle the rest of the afternoon until the fire died. In unison, we turned back, walking towards our vehicles.

Cade glanced my way. "You want to grab a beer after work today?" he asked.

My usual answer would be yes. I wouldn't even have to think about it. But today I had to think about Maisie's dad. I'd dropped him off with the police chief, who happened to be Cade's father, hours ago. I knew I was about to walk straight into the buzz saw of gossip in Willow Brook. Not that Cade was much for gossip. In fact, he fucking hated it. He'd been burned pretty badly by gossip years back when he and Amelia first broke up.

I glanced his way and shook my head. "Nah. I've actually got something to take care of," I explained, hewing to the vague and hoping that might be enough.

Cade arched a brow. "Oh?"

I steeled myself. If there were one friend I'd confide in, it would be Cade, so I might as well just take it on the chin.

"Yeah, Maisie's dad showed up out of the blue today. Far as I can tell, he's here to mooch money off of her. I actually lassoed your dad into helping me out. Her dad doesn't have a car, and I didn't want him hounding her all day, so I dropped him off at the station. I thought your dad would be at the training exercise this morning and that would keep them tied up." I chuckled. "Your dad was a good sport about it. I gotta check back in with Janet, make sure she's got a room for him. Hopefully, I can persuade Maisie to let me buy him a plane ticket to leave tomorrow."

We'd reached our trucks by this point where they were parked side-by-side. Cade leaned his hips against the bumper on his and stared at me, his mouth agape. He gave himself a little shake, closing and then opening his eyes.

"What the fuck is going on?" he asked. "I kinda thought you had a thing for Maisie, well, for a while now. But I'm not sure how we got from that to you helping her deal with her dad. Not to mention, I don't know much about her dad but my mom says he's a loser."

I chuckled. "Pretty sure he's a loser. I'd heard as much from my mom years back." I paused and considered what to say next. Cade was no idiot, and he'd guess if I didn't fill him in. "What's going on with Maisie is we're seeing each other. I guess."

Cade's eyes widened slightly and then a slow grin stretched across his face. "Damn. I'll win this bet with Amelia."

"What bet?" I asked.

"Oh, I told her a while ago I thought you

had a thing for Maisie. She didn't believe me."

Fuck. I didn't want to worry about anyone getting nosy about Maisie and me. I wasn't worried about Cade in particular, but news traveled like a brush fire through Willow Brook. It actually mattered to me—a lot—how Maisie felt about this. I looked over at Cade, leaning a hip against my bumper and resting my elbow on the hood.

"Do me a favor. Don't mind if you mention it to Amelia, but ask her to keep it quiet. Maisie's gonna stress. She thinks if anyone knows what's going on it'll affect how the other guys see her."

Cade eyed me, his grin fading. He nodded. "Understood, man."

He was quiet for a few beats. I rolled my shoulders. I'd come to a place in my own mind about Maisie, but it wasn't something I'd quite sorted out how to talk about.

Cade gave me a long look before he spoke. "Well, about damn time as far as I'm concerned."

"What do you mean?"

"Just that. You've been playing the field for years. You're not an asshole, you're just the worst flirt I've ever known. I figured it was a matter of time until you found the right woman."

My heart twisted in my chest, the way I'd come to know it was wont to do whenever I thought much at all about how I was starting to feel about Maisie. My muddled feelings must've shown on my face.

He continued, "I figured you'd eventually settle down. That's all I meant."

All kinds of questions tumbled through my mind, none of which I was ready to ask just yet. So I nodded. "Okay. Well, I'm off to go find your dad and Janet and figure out what to do with Maisie's dad. Should be an interesting afternoon," I said.

Cade pushed away from his truck with a laugh. "I'll say. Catch you later then. Let me know if you need anything."

"You got it."

We respectively drove away with me heading straight for the station. Within moments, I walked into Chief Masters office. The police station was connected to the fire station, but the entrance was on the other side of the building. I found Maisie's dad sitting in a chair in the waiting area. He was flipping through a magazine. He glanced my way when I came through the door, nudging his chin up.

"Hey there. You here to pick me up?" he asked.

"Sure thing. Give me a sec. I need to check in with the chief."

Hank simply looked back down at his magazine and kept on flipping the pages. I rapped sharply on the chief's office door. At his call for me to come in, I stepped inside, closing the door behind me. Cade was a ringer for his dad. Rex Masters had the same curly brown hair, although it was now streaked with gray. His face was weathered, and he always had a ready grin. At least for me, he did.

"Here to take over babysitting duty?" he asked with a grin.

I chuckled. "That's exactly why I'm here. Anything I should know?" I asked.

Rex shook his head. "Nope. Rather uneventful day. I thought about bringing him down to the training exercise early, but my shift isn't up for another hour. I figured you might want to avoid the questions his presence might bring."

I'd filled Rex in this morning. He was in full agreement that Hank should skedaddle from Willow Brook as soon as feasibly possible. As he put it, the only good thing he knew about Hank was he was a killer poker player.

As if Rex read my mind, he said, "I've been thinking about your worry he's trying to mooch cash off of Maisie. Take him down for a poker game at Wildlands tonight. If he's as good as he was twenty years ago, he'll probably clean up. The blow will be easier when Maisie tells him she's not gonna bail him out of whatever money he owes now."

I angled my head to the side and nodded. "Excellent plan. Should've thought of it myself."

Rex chuckled. "Well, I'm a problem solver, that's my main job description. But I was also around when he swept through town and took Maisie's mom with him. He was here for a few weeks. You know I like my cards, so I ran into him at the bars back then. He knows his way around a poker game. Seems to take pride in it," he said.

"It's not my idea of a fun night, at least not with him, but I'll do it. You should've seen the look on Maisie's face when she opened the door and he was standing there. What else do you know about him?" I asked.

I hadn't had a chance to talk at length with Janet today. She would know the whole scoop, far more than my haphazard memories from bits and pieces that I overheard my mom talking about when I was younger. Everybody had been close to Carol, so they were all protective of her after her daughter had moved away and then never returned. It had broken Carol's heart, and I couldn't help but wonder if Maisie's mom eventually would've moved back if she hadn't died. But she had, and that made returning impossible—completely and forever.

Rex leaned back in his chair and ran a hand through his hair. "Georgie will know," he commented, referring to his wife. "I gave her a call today and made her swear up and down not to start spreading rumors about you and Maisie."

I hadn't offered any explanation to Rex, but there weren't many reasons for why I would've been at Maisie's house at the crack of dawn this morning. I wished I'd had a chance to talk to Maisie before her dad had shown up. I wanted to tell her to forget trying to keep everything a secret. But, I knew damn well she'd have some feelings about that.

Once upon a time, I would've, but now I didn't give a damn. Actually, all I wanted was to be with her. While I hadn't faced it fully just yet, I knew with close to certainty something had shifted for me with Maisie. The word *love* danced along the edges of my thoughts. I pushed back against it a little. While I might be ready to say I couldn't imagine being with anybody else now that I'd been with Maisie, I wasn't quite ready to say I was in love with her. Damn close though. I glanced to the floor, staring at the toes of my battered leather boots for a few beats before looking back over at Rex.

"Thanks for that. As I'm sure you can see, things have kinda moved along with her."

In a flash, I remembered that Maisie had this worry that I was somehow partially her boss. I figured it would be best if I spoke to Rex about that sooner rather than later. He wasn't my boss, but he was Maisie's boss. I took a breath and steeled myself. I'd convinced myself so thoroughly it wasn't a problem for Maisie and me to be together that I was currently realizing I might've been avoiding a potential problem.

"Tell me something," I said.

Rex was quiet and arched a brow. "Tell you what?" he asked.

"Am I Maisie's boss in some sort of sideways way?"

That got me a loud bark of a laugh from Rex, which quickly morphed into a long bout of laughter. He propped his elbow on his desk and rested his chin in his hand, shaking his head slowly.

"I was wondering when you were gonna ask that," he said.

A hint of worry flashed through me. Not because I didn't think we could sort this out, but because I knew Maisie would freak.

"So?" I asked.

Rex's eyes were twinkling, and I sensed he was enjoying my discomfort. "I'm the only boss of Maisie around here. No need to worry there. Since a few of you are crew superintendents, I suppose if I was gone, I could technically ask you to cover for me and then you'd be her boss. Unless I do that, you're not her boss. There are a few rules around inter-office relationships though," he added, using air quotes with the expression.

"Ohhh-kaay, what are those?" I asked.

Rex chuckled again. "I could screw with you on this one, couldn't I?"

I sighed and gave him a beseeching look. "You could, but please don't. Just give me the lowdown."

"Fair enough. The rules are you need to let me know because I'm the only chain of command person around here. I'm not even technically your boss but you answer to me as far as station matters go. Consider me told. The next step is Maisie has to let me know she's cool with it."

I stared at him, abruptly realizing my mouth had actually dropped open. I snapped it shut.

"Are you serious? You have to have a conversation with her about this?"

His grin widened again before he nodded firmly. "Damn straight I do. How you think that'll go?" he asked.

I rolled my eyes. "How do you think it'll go?" I asked, my voice actually cracking a little with my words.

Fuck fuck fuck. This is gonna go over just great.

Rex threw me a wry look. "We've got some time. How about you talk to her about it? I'm guessing you have already."

I shook my head.

He seemed to take pity on me finally, based on the look on my face. "Deal with her dad first and then talk to her about this. Just so you know, it's not like I couldn't guess what was going on."

I stared at him, my mouth dropping open again. "What?"

That only got me another laugh.

Rex shook his head slowly. "Beck, I've

been around the block many, many times. I'm pretty observant. You look at that girl like she's the center of the universe, and she does her damnedest not to look at you."

I silently groaned, mentally adding another thing to my list of not-great-shit-to-deal-with-this-week. "Well, thanks for covering for me with Georgie. I'm off to deal with Maisie's dad. Don't suppose you'd want to join us for a poker game at the bar tonight?"

Rex smiled widely at that. "I'd love it. Text me when you're on the way."

At that, I turned on my heel and left, throwing another thanks over my shoulder as I headed out the door. I collected Hank and headed over to Firehouse Café. Janet owned the café and an attached building where she ran a small summer B&B. I had to sort out whether Janet had a room for Hank, get a hold of Maisie, and deal with the plane ticket if she'd let me. On top of that, now I was playing poker tonight.

Chapter Twenty-Five

MAISIE

Later that night, I watched as Beck walked away with my dad trailing behind him. I couldn't quite believe it, but apparently they were playing poker. According to Beck, this was the brainchild of Chief Masters. It was brilliant actually. For the first time ever, I hoped my Dad cleaned up. I wanted him to have enough money to have a little cushion when he got back home.

I recalled Beck's explanation. *This way, he'll earn a little cash and it'll ease the pressure on you. That's all I'm after.*

I still didn't quite know how to accept Beck's support like this, but he was making it all but impossible to refuse, not to mention Janet had corralled me into a corner over it. I leaned back into my chair at Firehouse Café and looked over at Janet and Amelia. Janet had seen fit to bring in reinforcements this evening. Dinner with my dad had consisted of me, my dad, Janet and Amelia. Beck had shown up towards the end to fetch my dad for the planned poker game. Amelia looked from me to the door right when Beck looked over his shoulder once more. His eyes caught mine. Just that one look and his gaze pierced me across the room. It felt like a flame licked through the air between us. He stood holding the door for a few beats longer than would've been expected, tearing his eyes away at the last second and stepping through quickly. The bell jingled behind him as he disappeared.

I leaned back into my chair, pressing my thighs together to ease the sudden ache there. This was fucking ridiculous. I should've been rattled and disconcerted with the last thing on my mind being sex. Instead, all I could think about was sex, well specifically sex with Beck. It didn't help matters that I was also in a crowded café. I snatched my coffee off the table and took a big gulp, the bitter flavor grounding me slightly and distracting my attention from the need burning through me. After I set my coffee down, I glanced between Janet and Amelia.

"Whoa," Amelia said.

Janet chuckled.

"Whoa what?" I asked.

Amelia twisted her mouth and rolled her eyes. "Oh. Just that I thought you two were gonna set this room on fire there. I lost a bet with Cade over you and Beck by the way," she said with a slow shake of her head.

"What do you mean you lost a bet?"

Amelia laughed a little. "A while ago, Cade said he thought Beck had a thing for you. I told him he was crazy. Not to mention, I really didn't think you'd go for it."

I suddenly felt a little defensive. But I didn't say anything. She must've picked up on something in my eyes because her gaze sobered.

"Don't get me wrong, you're awesome, and Beck is too. We grew up together. I always figured it was just a matter of time before he settled down a little bit. I don't want you to take this the wrong way, but you used to be kind of, well, cranky. It didn't seem like you'd be interested in anyone, least of all Beck. He's pretty happy-go-lucky. Now that I've gotten to know you a little, I know you're not cranky you're just..."

"Bitchy?" I offered helpfully.

Janet burst out laughing. "Bitchy fits."

Amelia laughed with us and then sobered again. "I guess I'd say you were kinda guarded, or something."

"Well now that you met my dad and a little bit about what he was like, I suppose you can see why. I'm not used to anybody having my back," I explained.

Janet reached over and squeezed my shoulder. "Plenty of us have your back."

My throat tightened, but I swallowed and took a breath. "It's kind of weird actually." I didn't say aloud how unsettling it was. All day I'd been shadowboxing in my mind. One minute, I wanted to let Beck take care of me. The next minute, I was annoyed and frustrated with the feeling. I couldn't trust myself enough to relax and let go.

I took another sip of coffee. Amelia's gaze was considering.

"Back to my point. Wow you two are hot for each other!"

Janet laughed again, and I couldn't help but laugh myself. Amelia was quite right. I didn't want to talk much about it because I didn't really know what to do with the bundle of feelings that I held inside about Beck.

"I'm worried if the guys at the station find out, it'll be weird."

My words escaped before I really thought about them.

Amelia cocked her head to the side. "I can see why you might worry, but I think it'll be fine. Willow Brook is small for the locals no matter what, so gossip is part of life. I've been through the ringer on it. I'm no fan of it myself, so you can trust me to keep quiet. But if I noticed the way you two were looking at each other, you can be pretty damn sure other people have too."

I took another gulp of coffee. "Right. Well, I need to sort out this thing with my dad right now. One thing at a time. It's not like anything's official with Beck anyway."

Janet glanced my way, her eyes narrowing.

"What's that for?" I asked.

"It's pretty official. When Beck is your dad's taxi, he's planning on buying a plane ticket for him, and he's the one who ran around town this morning rallying me up to find a room for him and the police chief to be his babysitter all day, it's not just a fling," she said pointedly.

I stared at Janet, my cheeks getting hot. When she said it like that, I suppose it did seem like Beck and I were something more. I didn't know what to think, but I was a specific person. I needed things spelled out for me. Perhaps it was the chronic uncertainty that I'd lived with as a child. I liked lists and forms, things that were really clear, that meant certain things were going to happen. I supposed I needed to talk to Beck, but I didn't even know where to start. My past relationships had been short-lived. The fumbling mess that high school and college generally were. They just sort of happened and then I moved on. Anxiety coiled in my belly.

Chapter Twenty-Six

BECK

I leaned back in my chair as Hank played his last hand. Rex had been spot on, Maisie's dad was a helluva poker player. I didn't normally enjoy losing. I liked to win, even if I only played cards for fun. It was nice to take home a little extra cash. No such luck tonight. Instead, I was relieved because Hank had made a tidy little profit for himself. I had no idea how much cash he had intended to try to weasel out of Maisie. Yet, I hoped the few hundred he'd won tonight would be enough to carry him over once he landed back in California. The one piece of the puzzle I hadn't sorted out yet was getting him on a plane tomorrow. When I tried to talk to Maisie about it again earlier today, she'd been wishy-washy. So I'd held back.

I watched while Hank joked around with a few of the other guys at the table. Aside from Hank's presence, tonight was a fairly typical evening for me at the bar. There was one glaring difference—I'd hardly been here since I'd started seeing Maisie. I took a long drag off my beer. I heard my name and glanced over my shoulder. I saw Janice approaching out table. Janice wasn't from Willow Brook yet she was often in the area. She spent summers between here and Anchorage. Her parents owned a hunting lodge in Willow Brook. She and I had seen each other casually off and on over the years. I gave her a little wave and then looked back towards the table. It wasn't that I was purposely trying to cut her, but I didn't think much of it. It wasn't like we'd ever been serious. In fact, I'd only dallied with her when I wasn't having another short-term fling. Because short-term flings were all I did. Except for Maisie.

I heard my name again and glanced up to realize Janice had threaded her way through the crowd and stopped by the table, resting her hand on my shoulder. I rolled it slightly, trying to dislodge her hand without being obvious. This was an odd situation for me. Normally, I'd think nothing of it if she wanted to flirt a little even if I was tied up with somebody else. But now, there was Maisie. I wasn't so much worried what anybody thought because there was nothing untoward happening. Yet, it just didn't feel right.

"Hey Beck, how's it going?" she asked.

I purposely leaned forward to pointlessly reach for a napkin from the center of the table, effectively forcing her hand off my shoulder.

"Nothing much. Just a game of cards with some friends," I replied.

She glanced around the table, flashing a grin at the collective group.

"Who won tonight?" she asked.

Rex laughed and nudged his thumb towards Hank. "Hank's the winner tonight. We're just winding down. You around for a little bit?" he asked conversationally.

While Janice's parents didn't live in Willow Brook, and neither did she, her family was known around town. Families like hers were affectionately known as 'snowbirds.' They tended to come in for the summer and then leave every winter. Her parents stayed in Willow Brook occasionally, while she stayed in Anchorage most of the summer with a weekend here or there in town.

"Just for a long weekend," she replied. "How have you been?" she asked.

Rex launched into a meandering update of his summer.

A slight sense of relief rolled through me. I didn't know if Rex was doing it on purpose, but he'd effectively drawn her attention away from me. About then, I heard someone say Cade's name and glanced over to see Amelia approaching with Maisie at her side. A little buzz of electricity jolted through me. Seeing Maisie brought an instant smile, and my body tightened with need.

They approached the table, Amelia immediately moving to Cade's side and dropping her head to kiss him. It was slightly awkward to have Janice still standing there right at my side. I was tucked in the corner in such a way that no one else could stand at my side. I experienced an odd mix of feelings. I wanted to stand and push Janice out of the way, so I could pull Maisie into my lap and kiss her senseless. In this moment, I was frustrated Maisie and I had been keeping everything on the down low so far. I had a feeling she wouldn't appreciate it if I greeted her publicly the way I wanted. It didn't really matter because it was impossible to do without making a scene with Janice at my side.

Rex caught my eyes as he carried on his conversation with Janice and then pushed his chair back and stood. "Well guys, I'm gonna head home. Georgie'll expect me anytime now. I don't want to be too late seeing as I don't even have any winnings to show for tonight," he said with a low chuckle.

Rex standing effectively got the rest of the group to start shifting. Unfortunately for me, Janice didn't seem to get the cue. Even though I was paying little attention to her, she kept lingering.

"So what's your schedule tomorrow?" Cade asked conversationally, his question entirely pointless as he and I had confirmed our schedules earlier.

I sensed he was trying to make sure I didn't get accidentally trapped alone with Janice and Maisie. I had enough sense to know Amelia probably knew what was up by this point as well. She dragged Janice into some conversation about hiring at her parents' lodge, which finally got Janice to stop lingering at my side.

Maisie was quiet, which wasn't particularly surprising. She generally was. Once

Janice was distracted, I allowed myself a moment to look at Maisie. Damn. She was beautiful. Her brown curls were loose, a wild tumble around her shoulders. My heart clenched at seeing the carefully guarded look in her wide brown eyes. My body tightened as I let my gaze drift over her. She wore a V-neck t-shirt. My mouth watered at the thought of dragging my tongue down between her breasts. I forced my gaze up, only to land on her full lips. Fuck me. My control was shredded when it came to her. There was no such thing as casual appreciation with her.

All I wanted to do was drag her to me and kiss her senseless. For a flash, I considered doing just that anyway. I had to force myself to look away. Her father said something and then decided to be funny and piss me off.

"Your boy here knows his way around the cards. If only he hadn't been so distracted by all the girls, I might not have been able to beat him so easy," he said with a laugh.

Maisie glanced to him and then back to me. After a moment, she laughed a little, the sound forced, and then looked away from me to her father.

"So how'd you do?" she asked.

"Decent. I'll need a little more, but another few nights, a little help from you, and I'll be good to go," he replied.

The casual expectation in his tone infuriated me, but now wasn't the time. Maisie crossed her arms over her chest, her expression tight. She felt like she was a million miles away. I didn't know what the hell had flipped in her mind, but she'd pulled back so far, it felt as if she'd put an actual wall between us. I felt slightly panicked inside, but my hands were fucking tied with us surrounded by people.

Chapter Twenty-Seven

MAISIE

I kept my eyes away from Beck. My dad's comment had made my gut tighten and reminded me of everything I'd been conveniently ignoring about Beck. Of course, he'd be flirting and distracted.

I fiddled with my bracelet and then with the hem of my t-shirt, shifting my weight from foot to foot. I was uncomfortable in my skin. It was bad enough to be dealing with my dad here. I loved my dad. I really did. He just made me tired—his antics were so repetitive and always had been. So there was that. And then there was Beck. This whatever-the-hell we had going on was making me crazy. When it was just us, I could forget about what it meant outside of us. Yet, it had snowballed into something so much more, and I didn't know what to do about any of it. It was awkward to be here with him. This was his territory, not mine. My dad's comments had brought reality crashing down on me. I might not have been thinking about it consciously, but right now I realized I'd been letting myself get wishful. That needed to stop. Now.

When I'd been walking in with Amelia, it had been obvious that Janice was flirting with him. I presumed she was one of many women he flirted with. I might've shoved it to the back of my mind, but I hadn't forgotten he had a well-known reputation as a flirt and a playboy.

I stood there awkwardly, while she chatted up pretty much everybody at the table, her body language shielding Beck. I twirled a lock of hair around my finger. I was jumping from one nervous habit to another. My stomach coiled tighter with anxiety, and I felt slightly sick. This was the thing, even though I could kind of try to convince myself that Beck and I had something, I wasn't stupid. I knew I was nothing like most of the women he got involved with.

Maybe we had chemistry, maybe we had more than that. It didn't matter when I didn't know what he wanted. More importantly, I didn't know what I wanted. We were at a crossroads, and I didn't know how to handle it. The easy answer, the answer I wanted to be right, was to simply let things keep going as they were. It was too delicious to be with him, so tempting I could hardly stay away. But, if I let things keep going, I was moving into a danger zone. Knowing that my heart was already in a more fragile place than I'd ever wanted or anticipated, I could hardly bear to think how I might shatter if I let myself get hurt. If I took control, I could perhaps soften the blow. I didn't want to think about how taking control was the way I protected myself. It was all I knew how to do.

With everybody gradually filtering away from the table and Cade and Amelia lingering and making small talk, Janice was nudged away from Beck's side. I was relieved at that.

It doesn't make a damn difference. Are you going to suddenly latch onto him now?

My snide side just had to get that little dig in.

Everything that was happening with us had been tucked into the shadows of my life. The fact it was slightly out in the open now with Janet and Amelia brought it into stark relief. I stood there, switching from twirling one lock of hair to another, fiddling with my bracelet, adjusting my shirt, and managing to make polite chit chat, all the while fortifying my resolve inside.

My dad was joking around about how long he was planning to stay in Willow Brook. That made me uncomfortable too. I didn't like thinking about the fact that a big part of me preferred to keep him at a distance. I couldn't imagine my dad changing much at this point in his life. His life was one haphazard event after another. He wasn't a horrible man. It wasn't like he beat me or was abusive. It was years and years of benign neglect and a life of messy chaos. I knew it meant that if he actually lived close to me, I would experience more of that. Unlike down in California, the ripples of his life would spread much farther here. Willow Brook was so small. In California, I'd been able to move five towns away. Even though it was only thirty miles away, he had plenty going on to keep himself otherwise occupied. Here, having my dad nearby would make it far harder to keep the clear boundaries I needed with him to stay sane.

Unfortunately, as we continued to linger, a few other women came along and flirted with Beck, hammering the point home that this was the guy he was—an easy-going flirt. His nickname Funtime Fireman was well earned, and I knew it. I hadn't let myself think it consciously, but as I stood there, I realized I'd had this tiny, quiet hope that maybe because of the way I felt when I was with him something more could come of it. I needed to get a clue. Tonight might be the ideal time.

I almost laughed watching Amelia try to run interference. She managed to chase off one woman after another. Eventually she elbowed Cade in the side. "Let's get the hell out of here," she said, her eyes flicking from me to Beck. "We can head to our place if you'd like."

Beck spoke up quickly. "I need to drop Hank off."

"Hey, if we're gonna keep playing cards, I'm game," my dad piped in.

That is the last thing I want to deal with. A longer night of this.

My heart twisted when Beck slid his arm around my shoulders. "Nah, I think we'll call it a night. I'll drop you off," he said with a nod to my dad.

He glanced down to me. My pulse had lunged the second he touched me. Around him, my body was always on high idle, just waiting for something to hit the gas pedal. His touch floored it. Yet, I steeled myself against it. I hated how out of control I felt around him.

"Amelia's taking me home," I announced abruptly, swinging to look her way.

She looked slightly surprised, but she covered it well with a quick nod. "Yup! You're Hank's taxi, and I'm Maisie's."

I slipped out from under Beck's arm, giving a little wave before almost running out of the bar. Amelia was gracious enough to stay quiet for the first few minutes of our drive. She came to a stop at one of the few stoplights in Willow Brook. There was a line of campers in front of us, which meant we'd be taking our sweet ass time on the five-mile drive to my house. Campers crowded the typically clear highways of Alaska all summer long.

Amelia turned to look my way, her perceptive gaze making me shift in my seat.

"For the record, I don't mind getting any of my friends out of a bind, but what the hell is going on?" she asked.

Before I had a chance to reply, she continued, "I mean, Beck is somehow in charge of dealing with your dad. Which you don't seem to mind, by the way. But you could hardly get away from him fast enough. With the way you were looking at him earlier, I figured you'd stopped fighting with yourself about him. What gives?"

I looked forward, wishing like hell we weren't sitting stuck behind a camper. If we weren't, Amelia would have to pay attention to the road. Instead, we inched forward when the light changed and then came to another stop.

My stomach was churning, and my heart hurt a little.

"Well?"

Okay, so my friendship with Amelia might be on the new side, but she was proving my judgment about her to be accurate. She used to intimidate the hell out of me, what with the fact she was about as badass of a woman as I'd ever seen. I'd come to learn she was friendly, warmhearted and the kind of friend who had your back. She also didn't let up when she had a question.

"Fine. Sure, we have a thing. I like him. A lot. But it's crazy. I mean, I'm nothing like the women he usually gets involved with. I don't think I can handle it if I let things go much further and then it all blows up in my face. If there's one thing I'm good at, it's being alone," I explained, flinching a little at the stoic tone of my voice.

The light changed again, and Amelia looked ahead. This time two whole campers made it through the intersection before we had to stop again. Amelia looked back to me, her hand resting atop the steering wheel.

"So you're scared then," she said.

It wasn't a question, more of a statement.

I felt myself getting annoyed. To be honest, I felt downright bitchy. This was my go-to place inside, the place where I felt like I had control.

"I'm not scared," I protested, looking away from her to stare out the window.

It was going on ten o'clock and the long, slow dusky evening was reaching its end. Denali rose tall in the distance, a beacon on the horizon. The sun had left streaks of deep red and orange in its wake. My heart was banging hard and fast in my chest, and my stomach hurt. The intensity of my feelings for Beck was too much, like a wave crashing over me and sweeping me out to sea. Though it wasn't quite the same, the loss of control was similar to how I'd felt for my entire childhood. I'd achieved a sense of stability and peace in the shifting sands of my life by making a place for myself here—alone—in Willow Brook, and away from the chaos my father left in his wake.

I didn't want to invite any kind of chaos back into my life.

It's different with Beck. It feels good. Really good.

Sex is what feels good. The rest is a big mess.

Amelia's breath came out in a slow sigh. The light changed again, and this time we got through. She turned onto the highway, quiet for a few moments.

"It sounds like maybe you should actually talk to Beck," she said as we passed by a field with the silhouettes of two moose in the distance.

"Talk?" was my brilliant response.

"Yes, talk. Look, I get why you might be worried. This is definitely not what Beck usually does. But he doesn't usually date anyone. He has these off the cuff flings that never last more than a week or two. I've known him since we were little. I can tell you he has *never* looked at anyone the way he looks at you. Just don't slam the door on it without at least trying to talk it through. Trust me, I did that once and it was the biggest mistake of my life."

"What do you mean?"

She turned down the road leading to my

house, flicking her eyes to me and back to the road.

"Well if you didn't hear the rumor mill cranking away when Cade first moved back to town, we'd had an ugly break up over gossip gone wrong. I could've saved myself seven years of missing him and almost being stupid enough to marry someone else if I'd talked to him," she said bluntly.

"Yeah, but it's not like Beck and I have anything like you and Cade," I countered quickly, too quickly.

She turned down my driveway and rolled to a stop in the circle in front of the house. Angling toward me, she arched a brow.

"You've got an answer for everything. Well, it's up to you. All I'm saying is I think Beck's worth it. I promise I wouldn't say a damn thing if I didn't see the way he looked at you."

My throat was tight with emotion. I swallowed and tried to breathe it away, but it wasn't budging. I finally nodded. "Okay. I'll think about it." I paused, staring out the window and watching the shadow of a bird shift across the ground just beyond her headlights.

"Thanks for the ride home," I said.

"Anytime. Call if you need anything."

Even that casual comment felt loaded. She couldn't know how hard it was for me to allow anyone to be there for me. I managed to thank her for the ride and say goodbye. I climbed out and walked onto the porch beside the kitchen, turning to watch her tail-lights disappear down the driveway, the little red lights glimmering in the wispy, almost-darkness.

I walked into my quiet house. For a moment, I was relieved. It was just me. I thought about taking a bath to unwind. The moment was followed with a piercing sense of loneliness. How could Beck have knocked through my defenses so ruthlessly fast? He'd only spent a few nights here, and I missed him acutely.

I gave myself a shake and straightened my shoulders. This would pass. It would have to. I stomped upstairs, annoyed with myself and the precarious state of my heart.

Chapter Twenty-Eight

BECK

I jogged up the steps on the side porch at Maisie's house, knocking quickly on the kitchen door. I'd dropped Hank off and raced out here. I'd be damned if I was going to let her blow me off. When she didn't answer, I raised my hand to knock again just as the door swung open. She stood there, her features tense and her eyes angry.

"Maisie, what the hell is going on?"

"Nothing," she replied flatly.

I was scrambling in my mind, trying to get a foothold on whatever had shifted between us. It didn't help that I'd had zero experience with this kind of situation. I never let things go far enough with any woman to have to worry about emotional misunder-standings, or whatever this was.

"Everything was fine this morning. I know things were nutty today with your dad around, but you seem pissed. At me."

She shrugged, her expression giving nothing away.

"Everything is still fine. Let's just say I came to my senses. I appreciate your help with my dad today, but I have to take care of him myself."

My heart was pounding so hard it hurt, and I felt slightly sick. I also felt panicked. I didn't panic. Ever. But she was shutting me out, and I didn't know why.

"If everything's fine, then I suppose I can come in," I countered, unable to keep the hint of sarcasm out of my tone.

I was getting pissed. I doubted it would help, but anger was the only emotion that made sense right now.

Her eyes narrowed. "You can't come in. Look, tonight reminded me of some things. I need to take care of myself, and I need to stop being ridiculous about you. You know as well as I do, I'm nothing like most women you get involved with. I'd say you should head back to your distractions."

Her mouth twisted when she said 'distractions.' I knew she was referencing her father's cavalier comment about me being distracted. I was furious, if only because I hadn't been distracted. I sensed her father didn't want anyone too close to Maisie who might get in the way of his guilt-tripping her.

I stared at her. "What the hell, Maisie? You're not being fair."

She threw her hands up. "Stop it, Beck. Just stop it. This... this thing with us isn't serious and won't ever be. You're kidding yourself if you think it will be. Right now, I'm the flavor of the month for you. I can't..."

She paused and for a second I thought I saw tears in her eyes. I started to reach for her, but she swatted my hands away, shaking her head rapidly.

"I can't do this, Beck. I just can't."

At that, she shut the door in my face. I knocked again.

"Maisie, talk to me. Don't do this," I called, speaking into the damn door.

The only reply I received was the call of a raven nearby in the trees. After several futile minutes of knocking, I turned away. Part of me wanted to break down the door, but I needed to regroup. There weren't many things I was certain of, but I was confident

Maisie wouldn't respond favorably to me forcing her door down.

I left with my heart aching and my mind spinning over how to make this right with her.

———

I slammed my truck door behind me and walked through the cool drizzle into Firehouse Café. It had been two full days since Maisie had effectively told me to fuck off. I could push the issue if I wanted, but something told me she needed the space. I was an action kind of guy, or so I'd come to learn the last two days. For the first time in my life, I felt as if I didn't have control of a situation. As a firefighter, I was steeped in contingencies. When one plan was thrown awry due to elements beyond my control—the wind, the rain, a lightning strike—I simply moved on to the next plan.

Here I'd thought fighting wildfires deep in the wilderness was hard. I'd had little clue of what it felt to have my emotions held hostage. I hadn't anticipated what it would be like to hunker down in an emotional storm when I felt driven to do something, anything to create the outcome I wanted. At the moment, I wanted to storm over to Maisie's place and demand she let me back in.

And what, man? Let you back in, so you two can keep burning the sheets up? What else?

I nearly growled at that skeptical voice. I hadn't expected any of this to go the way it had. Yet, I'd come to terms with how much Maisie meant to me. Which was precisely why I was forcing myself not to pressure her. Not yet. If this went on much longer, all bets were off. The thing was, Maisie was *it* for me. Even contemplating a return to my days of a little fun here and there when I could find it made me restless and annoyed. I knew damn well all I'd be thinking about was Maisie and what I was missing. So here I was, hanging back and waiting. I knew I wouldn't wait too long, but for now, I figured it was best. Especially with Maisie's dad still around town.

I laughed to myself as I stepped into the café, my senses assailed by the scent of rich coffee, a variety of foods, and the contrasting warmth in here from the damp cold outside. I couldn't quite believe that most of my spare time the last two days straight had been spent mulling over the best way to approach Maisie. Worrying about what someone else might think wasn't something I did often.

Well, I wasn't worried about what she thought. I was worried about how she felt. That was a novel experience for me.

Work had kept my schedule busy. Our training exercises had been interrupted by a large fire on the outskirts of town. Some hikers passing through had stupidly violated the no-campfires rule in a reserve and set a dry section of the forest on fire. All of our crews had been busy in a round the clock rotation to deal with it. As a result, I hadn't even seen her at the station. My crew was on the early rotation, which was when she was working.

It was later afternoon now, I was tired, dirty, covered in soot and smelling like smoke. I was hoping to catch a few minutes to talk with Janet, along with grabbing a cup of my favorite coffee. I glanced around at the crowded café. This place was busy no matter what. Summers made it even more so with the tourists pouring into town. Throw some rain on their plans, and every store and restaurant in town was packed.

I headed for the back of the line at the counter. I'd only been there for a second when I heard my name. I glanced up to see Janet standing in the swinging doorway into the kitchen behind the counter.

"You got a minute?" she called.

"Of course," I replied.

She waved for me to follow her, so I stepped around the line and slipped behind the counter. The door swung shut behind us, muting the low hum of conversation in the café. Janet wore a flour-covered apron and promptly returned to whatever project she was working on in the bakery.

I leaned my hips against a counter running along the wall, facing the stainless steel table where she was working.

"Maisie's dad still staying here?" I asked, not bothering with the preliminaries.

Janet rolled her eyes and nodded. "Yes, I was actually planning to call you, so I'm glad you stopped by." She reached for a rolling pin to one side of the table and started methodically rolling out small circles of dough. "Hank seems to think he can stay here as long as he wants. I gotta tell you, I've known guys like him. Give them an inch, and they'll take twenty miles. I told him he's got until tomorrow and then the room is booked."

"Is it really?" I asked, torn between bitter laughter at how entitled Hank was and swearing at the effect it had on everyone around him.

Janet glanced up from what she was doing

with a quick grin. "Yes, it's actually booked. A family reserved it a few weeks back when they lost a reservation at another place nearby. He'll have to leave. Did you ever buy that ticket for him?" she asked.

I shook my head, my heart clenching painfully in my chest. Any reminder of Maisie made my heart ache. "No, Maisie wasn't ready for it, so I held off. Why'd you want to call me?" I asked.

"Well, for starters, what the hell is going on with you and Maisie now?"

I shrugged, my heart twisting a little more, my mind flashing to the closed, guarded look in her eyes the other night.

"I don't know," I said because there wasn't much else to say. "She won't talk to me."

"Dammit," Janet muttered under her breath as she set the rolling pin to the side and quickly dropped filling in the middle of a row of pastry circles. She looked back up at me while she worked. "She's not used to having anyone there for her. Her dad showing up is pushing all of those buttons. She might think she wants space, but I don't think that's what she needs."

"So you wanted to call me about Maisie?" I asked.

Janet shook her head. "Actually no. I

heard from my attorney, Robert Marsh, the one who set up Carol's will and trust for Maisie. He called me because she listed me as the back up power of attorney if needed."

My gut clenched, suspicion immediately entering my mind. God knows what Hank knew about Maisie's situation and everything she'd inherited from her grandmother.

"What did you hear from Robert?" I asked.

"Hank called over there. Hell if I know how he got Robert's name. Robert said Hank was asking all kinds of questions. I'm guessing he got wind that Maisie might've inherited that land and trust fund. My guess is he's hoping to hit her up for it," she said darkly.

I kicked my boot against the wall behind me. "Fucking asshole. This is exactly why I wanted him out of town as soon as possible. It's not that I don't want Maisie to have a chance to visit him. I can see she loves him, but he breaks her heart."

Janet nodded emphatically. "I know. That's exactly what I'm worried about."

"I'm not so sure I'm the best one to give Maisie a hint on this," I said.

Janet eyed me for a long minute. "You think not?" she asked.

A harsh laugh rumbled in my chest, a hint of bitterness rising with it.

"Look, I thought things were going somewhere with us. I know I'm no expert at this kind of thing..."

A small smile curled the corner of Janet's mouth. "No, you're probably not an expert."

"I'd love to let you lecture me right now," I said with a small chuckle. "...but we need to nip whatever Hank's doing in the bud."

She sobered, her eyes flashing with anger. Hell, anger was coiled tight in my gut just thinking Hank had gone to the trouble to track down the attorney who handled Carol's will. I didn't know the finer details, but I knew Carol had owned lots of land. Before her husband passed away, he'd bought up several large chunks of land in and around Willow Brook. Alaska might be wild, but land in this part of it was worth good money. Carol had left everything she owned to Maisie.

As I considered this, I rolled my head from side to side, trying to ease the tension bundled there. "I cannot fucking believe Hank went to the trouble to find out who handled Carol's will. What do you think he knows?"

"Well, Robert didn't tell him a damn

thing. He didn't even confirm he knew who Carol was. But who knows what Maisie's mom told him before she passed away? It's not like she'd have known how well her parents planning would pay off as far as investments and whatnot, but she knew how much land they owned. He was fishing for info, no other reason for him to be calling the attorney."

I kicked my heel against the wall behind me again, running a hand through my hair with a sigh. I was trying to imagine how it would go over if I inserted myself any deeper into this mess between Maisie and her dad. I kept picturing her face when he showed up at her door. The sad, weary frustration mixed with the heaviness of guilt. I thought about what I'd pieced together about her childhood since then. Realizing that she'd spent most of her life fending for herself. I wanted to act as her shield, but I knew it was important to her to stand on her own. It made me sick to realize how willing her father was to emotionally blackmail her just to get something out of her. Men like Hank skated through life by stumbling upon luck, and the begrudging help of others. I imagined he loved Maisie in his own haphazard way. But it was in his nature to always look for the easy way to score a buck. I looked back over at Janet.

"You talk to Maisie, and I'll talk to Hank. Do you think she even knows he's been nosing around about this?" I asked.

Janet shrugged. "I doubt it. It's not like she doesn't know how he is. But I doubt she thought he was savvy enough to dig around like this. She doesn't even know how much is in the trust fund that will eventually go to her. I'm damn glad Carol tied it up so tight legally. Otherwise, I imagine Hank would be knocking down doors to get to it. Robert said he was asking a lot of questions. Fortunately Robert had the sense to let Hank run his mouth without telling him a damn thing."

I took a breath and pushed my hips off the counter. "All right, I'm gonna grab a coffee before I leave. Do you know where Hank is right now?" I asked.

"He hasn't stopped over here yet, so he's probably still in his room. You know where to find him. I'll finish up here and go talk to Maisie in a little bit."

"Thanks for giving me a heads up. I'll let you know what Hank says. How bad do you think it would be if I went ahead and just bought the damn plane ticket and drove him

to Anchorage without letting Maisie know?"
I asked.

Janet rolled her eyes. "Not good. I'm gonna go talk to her. Don't worry, I'll take the blame for asking you to talk to her dad. I'll tell her I made you. I would've if you hadn't said yes."

I chuckled, a kind of sad laugh that was like a small knife to my heart, as I gave a wave and pushed through the swinging door out front. I felt so fucking protective of Maisie. I wanted to make this right for her, and I didn't even know if she would let us have a chance.

Chapter Twenty-Nine

MAISIE

I tapped to answer my call. "911, what's your emergency?" I asked.

"Hi Maisie, it's Carrie Dodge again."

Based on the tone of her voice, she sounded safe so I took that as a good sign.

"Hi Carrie, what can I do for you?" I asked.

"It's Herman again," she announced.

"Again?"

I bit back the urge to laugh. I knew she loved Herman, but I couldn't help but wonder what predicament he'd gotten himself into this time.

"Yes, now he's in a different tree. Do you think you can send the crew out? I hope it's

Beck's crew. He's my favorite," she said with a sly laugh.

My heart clenched in my chest. Beck was definitely my favorite too. In so many ways. It had been two full days since I'd told him to leave me alone. He'd been tied up dealing with a big fire on the outskirts of town, so I hadn't even seen him. I supposed it was a good thing he hadn't been around much. At least for me to stay sane. My heart might've shattered if I'd had to face him right away. I was a mess inside. It was causing me physical pain inside to keep my distance, but it's what needed to happen. Every time I thought about any other option, I reminded myself I didn't know what he wanted. If the past was any predictor of the future, I was probably a slightly longer than usual diversion for him and nothing more.

Emotion lodged in my throat, tightening my chest and almost taking my breath away. Every time I tried to convince myself that was how it was and why I needed to do what I was doing, I remembered how it felt to be with him. How it wasn't just sex or desire, how it felt as if we were being bound tighter and tighter, the ropes of intimacy twining around us. Then I would remind myself that was nothing more than my imagination. I was probably making it all up in my head. I forced my attention to my call with Carrie, managing to laugh a little with her about Beck being her favorite.

After radioing the crew, I confirmed with her they'd be there shortly and ended the call. I was instantly restless. I liked to work hard, but with Beck churning through my thoughts the last few days, I didn't enjoy any downtime at work. I spun around, looking back at the row of filing cabinets against the wall. About six months ago, Chief Masters had asked me to organize the last few decades of old files and transition the data into the new computer system. It was a big project and definitely something that would keep me busy for quite some time going forward. I looked up where I left off and got started, pulling the files out, scanning them in and entering the data into the system.

I was deep into the letter C at this point. It had taken me a full six months to get from A to C. The bell dinged above the entrance, and I spun in my chair, relieved to see it was only Janet. Lately every time somebody came in, I half hoped it was Beck even though it made no sense for him to come through the front entrance. That was how much I wanted it to be him.

"Hey Janet, what's up?" I asked, wheeling my chair back to face the front.

She walked to the counter and rested her elbow on it. "Well, I came to talk to you," she said.

My gut coiled. I didn't know what was up, but I'd been living with that low-level anxiety I always lived with whenever my dad was around. That anxiety was compounded right now with my mixed feelings about Beck and how much I missed him. I'd been working up the nerve to let my dad know that he needed to get on a plane and leave. I'd made the decision myself that I would buy his one-way ticket. He'd been dropping hints left and right that he was thinking about staying. I didn't think I could handle that. I needed the distance and to not feel like he was always looking for what he could get out of me.

Janet's eyes were a little sad and determined. She was quiet for a beat before she spoke. "I'll just get right to the point. Your dad's nosing around. He called Robert Marsh, the attorney that handled your Gram's estate for you, asking way too many questions. Robert obviously didn't give him any information, but he told me your dad must've looked up the old property records, because somehow he knows that you inherited several different parcels from her."

I felt sick and tired as hot tears pressed at the back of my eyes. Why oh why did my dad always have to do this? He seemed constitutionally incapable of not looking for what he could scam from somebody else. It didn't seem to matter that I was his daughter.

When I didn't say anything, Janet continued, "I also sent Beck to tell your dad to back the hell off. Before you go getting pissed at Beck, blame me. I know you love your dad, but he'll yank on those strings of guilt like nobody's business. I won't stand by and let him bully you just so he can score some extra money by selling off your properties. God help us if he finds out you have a trust fund waiting for you when you turn thirty-five. He'll stay here just so he's around when you have access to it. Beck will stand up to him and save you the trouble."

I stared at her for a minute before I realized my mouth had fallen open. Even though I'd pretty much told Beck to fuck off, he hadn't hesitated to help when Janet asked him to. A rush of emotion rose inside, and I burst into tears. I put my face in my hands and just sobbed. I heard Janet hurrying around the counter and pulling up a chair beside me.

She rubbed my back and clucked a little. I didn't even know what to do or say. After a few minutes, I straightened and dragged the end of my sleeve over my cheeks. Still rubbing my back, Janet looked around.

"Dammit, where are the tissues?" she muttered to herself.

I pointed to the top of the filing cabinets.

She hopped up and returned with the entire box. I tugged one out and blew my nose, taking several shaky breaths before I gathered the nerve to look at Janet again.

I felt like an idiot to fall apart like this. I didn't quite know what to do. I finally managed to look at her and found her warm eyes waiting.

"Tell me what you need," she said.

I took a deep breath and let it out in a sigh. "Don't worry…"

"Don't even try to tell me you plan to deal with this by yourself!"

Her eyes were flashing, and she looked genuinely offended.

"I wasn't going to say that. I was about to say don't worry about me getting upset about Beck. That's all. Honestly, it's fine if he talks to my dad."

As soon as I said that, a tight spool of tension unwound inside of me. I couldn't even wrap my brain about what it meant to stop fighting the tide of emotion inside of me. I didn't know what the future held, but I couldn't keep the walls up around my heart. No matter what, Beck was there for me. In ways I hadn't ever imagined anyone being there for me. The least I could do was not slam the door in his face, metaphorically speaking.

"Okay," Janet said slowly.

When I looked her way, I could practically see the wheels spinning in her brain.

"And then?" she asked.

"What do you mean?"

She sighed loudly and rolled her eyes. "I swear, you are purposefully obtuse sometimes. And then what about you and Beck?"

My cheeks got hot, and my heart spun a little. I was anxious and worried and didn't know what would happen next.

"We'll see what happens next. First, I need to say goodbye to my dad."

Chapter Thirty

BECK

"You can't tell me to leave. If Maisie wants me gone, she'll say so," Hank said, a hint of belligerence in his tone.

I'd encountered him on the short walk from the café to the cutesy B&B Janet owned beside it. As such, we were standing on the sidewalk on Main Street for this little conversation. I was fighting the urge to haul off and punch him when I heard someone call my name.

I glanced around and saw Maisie walking toward us from the direction of the station. I briefly wondered why she hadn't driven, but that mild curiosity was wiped away in the tidal wave of relief that washed through me when I saw her. Hell, it was so fucking good to see her. I completely forgot I'd been in the middle of confronting her dad and jogged to meet her. I forced myself to stop in front of her, holding back the urge to tug her to me and pour everything I felt into a kiss. It was still drizzling out, the sky slate gray and the air chilly.

Maisie's wild curls were damp and had fallen loose from her ponytail. Her thick lashes curled against her cheeks, which were flushed pink. She'd forgotten a jacket. I could see she was chilled with her nipples pressing against her t-shirt. She wrapped her arms around her waist. She hadn't said a word and just looked at me, her wide brown eyes coasting over my face. My heart set to thudding, and need lashed at me. It was pathetic really, how much of a hold she had on me.

I opened my mouth to say something, anything.

"I miss you," was the only thing that came out. My mouth was miles ahead of my brain and seemed stuck in the gear of blunt truth when it came to Maisie.

Her eyes widened and then suddenly she flung herself at me. I stumbled slightly as I caught her against me. I wrapped my arms around her and held on tight, tucking my head into the curve of her neck and breathing her in. She smelled of rain hinted with vanilla and the sweet scent that was only her. I dropped kisses along her neck, savoring the feel of her skin pebbling under my lips. My cock was rock hard, pressing against my zipper with raw, insistent need. I lost track of where we were until she wiggled against me, a little laugh escaping. I lifted my head to find her face inches away.

Her cheeks were cherry red now, her eyes glistening, and a lopsided smile unfurling across her face. She bit her lip, and I almost came undone.

This woman could bring me to my knees, and I didn't give a damn.

"Um, we're kind of..." she paused, gesturing with her hand.

I glanced around to see a few tourists walking by, their eyes curiously glancing to us and away. Her father had disappeared, and I found I couldn't seem to care about that right now.

"I suppose you'd rather I didn't tackle you right here in front of anyone who walks by," I said with a grin.

She lifted a shoulder in a shrug, the side effect of her breasts bouncing against my chest a major bonus. "Probably not."

I eased her down until her feet landed on

the ground, but I didn't loosen my hold. I brushed a damp curl off of her cheek. "Are we talking again?"

She sighed, but the little glint of joy in her eyes didn't fade. "I want to talk, but we need to deal with my dad."

For a second, I almost went along with her. But I held back. I needed her to know one thing for certain.

"He's not going anywhere."

She laughed a little at that, sadness flitting through the backs of her eyes.

There wasn't much space between us, but I pulled her a little closer as if I could ward off the world for her somehow if only I held her close enough.

"I missed you, and it was only two days. I had a lot of time to think," I began. My heart thudded even faster, but I forged ahead.

Janet's comment earlier that Maisie wasn't used to having anyone there for her had made me realize it might be pretty damn important for her to know I would. No matter what.

I might not have planned on falling for her—most assuredly not falling so hard I almost cracked my own heart open in the process—but I knew what it meant to be there for someone. I'd been lucky to witness my own parents who stuck with each other through thick and thin. It wasn't always perfect, but their love had been the glue that held them together.

"If you were wondering, I'm not going anywhere. Even if you shut me out, or I piss you off, I'll still be there. Waiting." I took a gulp of air, watching Maisie's eyes widen. "When I tried to think about moving on, I couldn't imagine it. That's when I realized I love you."

Her breath hitched and a tear rolled down her cheek, mingling with the soft rain falling on us. I brushed the tear away with my thumb, forcing myself to hold still, to let her absorb my words and respond however she did. With my heart banging away and emotion rushing through me, I clung to my patience and to the hope I hadn't pushed too far, too fast.

Another tear rolled down her cheek and she buried her face in my chest. Just as I was starting to think I'd blown this, she mumbled something and then looked up as if to gauge my response. Seeing as I hadn't heard what she said, I wasn't much help.

"I didn't hear you, babe. What was that?"

She bit her lip and sighed. "I said I love you too," she mumbled.

My heart felt like it was going to beat its way out of my chest. I didn't know what I was supposed to feel, but it was a rush of emotion and raw lust.

I sensed this wasn't easy for her. I couldn't say it was easy for me either. While I hadn't had much practice with this kind of love, well none to be honest, I knew what it meant to have people who were there for you. She didn't, so I sensed it was a risk she hadn't planned to take. Which made it all the sweeter.

I dipped my head, letting my forehead fall to hers. "Okay then," I said gruffly. "Now that we got that out of the way, I have one question."

"What's that?"

"Can I stay with you tonight?"

She nodded, her forehead bumping against mine slightly.

I didn't wait any longer and fit my mouth over hers. I meant for it to be a quick kiss, but the second her tongue slid against mine, I lost track of everything else. I poured days of pent up need and longing into her mouth. She didn't hold back either, twining her arms around my neck and kissing me as if I was the very air she needed to breathe. Her answering desire and entirely unrestrained response was like dropping a match in a vat of fuel. Our kiss went on and on—hot, wet, deep and raw sensory overload.

It wasn't until she shivered against me that I managed to draw back. Her lips were plump and swollen, her cheeks flushed and her skin damp from the drizzle. She was a bundle of softness in my arms, and all I wanted was to find the closest place to bury myself inside of her. Yet, reality intruded. We were in the middle of town. Even on a rainy day in summer, we had quite the audience.

I stepped back. "We need to get you somewhere dry," I said as I curled my hand around hers.

"We need to find my dad. I'm just going to keep worrying if I don't deal with him."

"So Janet talked to you?" I asked as I turned and started walking back toward Firehouse Café.

She nodded, that sad, weary look flashing through her eyes, reminding me I wanted to punch Hank.

"Yeah. I was already gearing up to get him a ticket, but him nosing around and trying to talk to Gram's attorney makes me want him out of here today."

"Want me to deal with him?"

She paused, stopping before we walked

into the café. Her eyes caught mine, and I saw the vulnerability there.

"I need to talk to him, but I don't mind if you're there. It'd be really great if you'd go with me when I take him to Anchorage. I could use some reinforcement."

I pulled her close and dropped a quick kiss on her lips. "Whatever you need."

Chapter Thirty-One

MAISIE

I stood on the sidewalk at the airport, waiting while Beck pulled my dad's bag out of the back of his truck. He handed it to my dad and caught my eyes briefly. I could see the unspoken question there. He was gauging whether I wanted him to wait in the car while I said goodbye to my dad. My heart gave a hard thump. I needed to say this goodbye on my own. I shook my head, just barely. He nodded and turned to say something to my dad, clapping him on the shoulder and then rounding the truck to climb into the driver's seat.

My tearful encounter with Beck earlier, and his gruff, heartfelt announcement that he loved me would have been overwhelming all by itself. But then, I'd scrounged up the nerve and faced my dad. I'd told him I loved him and always would, but that I wouldn't let him bounce in and out of my life at his leisure whenever he was looking for me to serve as his personal bank. I knew I could've handled it myself, but I didn't have words for what it meant to know Beck was there with me. Between his actions over the last few days, and Janet's little pep talk, I knew I wasn't alone. That was something I'd never experienced.

I'd held up in the face of my dad's annoying wheedling and insistence he'd only been checking in with the attorney to make sure I'd gotten everything I was due from Gram's will. When my dad had insisted he needed a coffee and stepped away to get one, Beck had offered to book my dad a ticket back to California today. The magic of smartphones made it so he had the confirmation before my dad even returned with his coffee.

My dad slung his duffel bag over his shoulder and walked to stand in front of me. His eyes met mine. I could sense him considering what to say, so I jumped in.

"Dad, I'm glad you're doing okay," I said. "I hope you can understand how I feel."

He was quiet and then he shrugged. "I suppose I do. It hurts a little, but..."

I cut in. "Dad, it hurts *me* to have you only come to visit when you want something from me."

That shut him up. I don't know what else he meant to say, but after a moment, he nodded. He leaned over and dropped a kiss on my hair, pulling me into a quick hug. "Your boy there made me promise to call before I visit next time. I will."

At that he turned away. My throat felt tight. I watched him go through the revolving door into the airport, my eyes tracking him until he disappeared into the crowd of travelers.

———

I dropped my keys on the counter once we stepped through the door into the kitchen. I was tired, the kind of tired that seeps into every corner of you. I kicked off my shoes and flicked the lights on, adjusting the dimmer so it wasn't too bright. I turned to see Beck locking the door behind us and kicking off his shoes. My heart squeezed and another wave of emotion rocked me. This afternoon I'd felt like a boat in the ocean during a storm, adrift on tides of emotion and rocked by events beyond my control.

We were just getting back from the drive to Anchorage to drop my dad off. The rain had gone from a drizzle to a heavy downpour on the way back to Willow Brook. I felt wet and bedraggled on top of it all.

Beck looked up at me, and my breath caught. He was so handsome, it almost hurt to look at him. With his black curls damp from the rain, his rich green eyes stood out. His mouth curled at one corner, and my belly executed a slow flip. I almost laughed aloud. Here I was, bone tired, weary and emotionally drained. Still, all he had to do was throw one of his dangerous grins about and I wanted him. Desperately.

"Shower," he said firmly.

Before I could reply, he lifted me into his arms and carried me upstairs.

"Are you seriously carrying me? I can walk, you know."

He grinned again, the heat in his eyes calling to mine. "I know you can. This just gives me an excuse to cop a feel," he said, squeezing my bottom.

My sex clenched, and the weight of the day fell away. Within minutes, we were in the shower, the steamy hot water pouring over us. I was covered in soap with water sluicing over me when I felt his hands slide down my sides from behind, coming around to cup my breasts.

His cock—its full, hard length—pressed against my bottom. I couldn't hold back the moan that escaped.

He thumbed my nipples and slid one hand down to cup my mound. Need roared through me as his fingers slid through the wet curls there and dipped into my folds. I was slippery wet, my channel aching for him to fill me. All the while, his lips meandered down the side of my neck, hot, wet kisses mingling with the water sluicing over my skin. He drew his tongue down my spine, pushing me toward meltdown territory. My knees buckled, but he had me, one hand coaxing my pussy open and my thighs apart and the other holding me firmly at the hip.

I caught my balance on the tiled wall, the coolness an anchor to the madness and need swirling inside. His fingers stroked into my channel. I was lost, adrift on nothing but sensation. Pressure coiled tighter and tighter. I felt his lips dallying over the curve of my bottom. He pushed my thighs further apart. He trailed kisses up the insides of my thighs where the skin was so sensitive, I cried out. His tongue trailed along my cleft and his fingers dallied there. A light brush across my clit, and I almost came. He drew back, heightening my need.

Another pass with his tongue, his fingers going deep. Then he buried his mouth between my thighs, spinning under me, so one of my legs hooked over his shoulder. I was bared to him, exposed in a way I'd never been. With his tongue working its magic and his fingers fucking me so slowly, I lost sight of everything but the intense sensation building inside. My channel started to convulse, another swirl of his tongue and then he sucked my clit into his mouth. Pleasure burst through me with such force, I screamed his name.

As the aftershocks rocked me, he eased away, carefully lowering my leg, his lips never breaking from my skin as he mapped his way back up my body. He paused to dally with my nipples—kisses, nips and light bites. Somehow he spun us around without me even noticing. The cool tile hit my back, and I sighed. I was barely able to stand. He lifted me against him, and my legs curled around his waist.

My body knew what I needed. Him. Buried inside of me.

"Maisie."

His voice was rough, but clear.

I opened my eyes to find his waiting. Once our gazes met, we were locked in. I couldn't look away, and I didn't want to. Need throbbed between us. I felt his cock at my entrance. It didn't matter that I'd just had an explosive orgasm. I needed him to be closer. I ached for it.

"Beck, please..." I murmured as I arched into him.

He didn't tease me for begging. His eyes darkened further and he lifted me slightly, adjusted his angle and sank inside, seating himself deeply. With our eyes locked together, he began to move, subtle nudges at first, each one deeper than the last. I was close, so close. This climax rose out of the aftershocks of the last. The pressure built and built as he surged into me again and again and again. The sound of the water cocooned us in an intense, wet dance of pleasure.

I chased after that sweet peak, that place where I could let go in only the way I could with Beck. He reached between us, pressing his thumb over my clit, so swollen with need. Once again, I was crying out, his name a shout. He followed me over, his body going rigid. I felt the heat of his release filling me and curled my legs tighter around him.

Not much later, I lay beside him in bed.

We were staring up at the skylight. Rain fell upon it, a soft patter in the darkness. I rolled to the side, curling against him, idly tracing circles over his heart.

"Thanks for today," I said, my voice low.

My need for Beck had held my weariness at bay for a little bit, but now it was crashing over me. I felt him shift and glanced up.

"For what?"

"For helping me with my dad. For... Well, for everything."

He was quiet, his gaze piercing me in the dim room, the only light cast from a small nightlight by my bed. "No thanks necessary."

His arm curled around my back, holding me close against his side.

"I love you," he murmured.

I swallowed against the tightness in my throat. Since I couldn't seem to speak, I pressed a kiss against his neck. I fell asleep, feeling warm, safe and not alone.

EPILOGUE

Beck

One year later

I walked across the dampened ground, blackened and charred trees with flames still flickering in the distance behind me. My crew was at the end of a rotation, helping manage a fire deep in the backcountry in Alaska. It had been a viciously exhausting two weeks. This part of the forest had been hit hard with spruce bark beetle, leaving far too much dry fuel for the fire. Our crew had spent the good part of two weeks establishing a solid firebreak to keep the fire at bay in the distance with several small Alaskan Native villages at risk from the fire. A hotshot crew from Fairbanks was flying in within the hour to pick up where we were leaving off.

I missed Maisie so much, my heart ached. Just as much, I missed our son Max. I still loved my job and always would. But I didn't love being away from them. I couldn't wait to get back home. These days home to me wasn't a place, it was Maisie and Max.

Not much later, I watched the landscape underneath the helicopter as we flew away. I looked over toward Denali in the distance, the anchor of the landscape in central Alaska. Clouds were arrayed around its peak. I took a breath, let it out and glanced at my watch. Maisie and I had developed the habit that we didn't bother trying to text when I was out in the field. It was too often nothing more than a source of frustration because I was almost never anywhere near cell reception.

The deal was once I was within a half-hour of Willow Brook, I'd text. A quick glance at my watch told me I was in the clear. I slipped my phone out, grinning the second I pulled up her name.

Tell me what you're wearing.

I immediately saw the little bubble appear, letting me know she'd been waiting. I fucking loved that.

OMG. You're ridiculous. You've been gone for two weeks and that's all you can think about?

I tapped out my reply quickly.

Absolutely. I've been gone for too long. That's exactly the point. Miss you.

She replied with a blushing, grinning emoticon.

Then a photo.

Fuck me.

The photo was of her cupping one of her breasts, the nipple taut and perky between her thumb and forefinger. My cock was hard instantly.

You're torturing me.

I could feel her giggling even though I was nowhere near her.

That's what you get for only thinking about sex. How long until you're home?

20 minutes.

K. I'll meet you there.

I put my phone away, my heart clenching the way it did whenever I was about to see her after I'd been away. We'd come a long way for two people who didn't quite know how to do relationships. Maisie still struggled to let me, or frankly anyone, be there for her, but she managed it. After a few months of me staying at her place every night, we'd finally made it official and I'd moved in. Not too long after that, we'd gotten married.

In short order, the helicopter came to a soft landing behind the station. I was in a rush to get out, solely because I couldn't get to Maisie fast enough. By the time I stepped out of the helicopter with my backpack over my shoulder, I looked ahead to see her holding Max as she stood just outside the garage. The wind caught her curls and blew them wild. She walked to meet me, and I caught her tight against my side, lifting Max from her arms and hugging them both. She dusted kisses all over my face. Damn, it was a relief just to hold her.

I couldn't imagine life without her. Trying to imagine that very circumstance was what had shown me I loved her.

"Good to be home," I murmured.

"Good for you to be home," she replied emphatically, her eyes bright and her smile wide as she pulled back.

Stepping back, she caught my hand in hers. "We're dropping Max off with Janet for a few hours. Let's go," she said with a sly grin.

I chuckled, knowing she had plans for us. "Want me to shower first?" I asked.

Whenever we returned from being out in the field, it was after weeks without anything even remotely resembling a shower. Perhaps a dip in a river, a lake, or whatever water we had on hand at camp, but that was it. I knew I was a little worse for the wear.

Maisie flashed a grin and shook her head, her curls swinging.

"Nope, let's go."

A brief drive later, after we had dropped Max off with Janet, we were home and she was tugging me into the shower with her. She was quick with the soap, sliding it all over me. With a chuckle, I pulled it from her hands as I stood under the shower with the water rinsing the soap away.

"What's the rush?" I asked.

She slid her hand down over my abs, curling it around my cock. I'd been at half-mast ever since she sent her naughty photo while I was flying back. I was instantly rock hard under her touch, aching for her. She looked up through her lashes with a grin. Before I had a chance to think, much less speak, she was kneeling down and dragging her tongue along the underside of my cock. She drew me into her mouth. My knees buckled slightly, and I slapped my hand behind me, steadying myself on the wall.

"Maisie," I choked out.

She hummed whatever she meant to say

around my cock, the subtle vibration sending a hot jolt of pleasure through me. I groaned, tangling a hand in her hair and surrendering myself to her ministrations. Two weeks without her had me burning up with need. I was at the edge before I knew it. I meant to say something, but I couldn't seem to speak. I gave her hair a little tug. She drew back to glance up. The brief pause helped me latch onto a thread of control. I tugged her up and out of the shower with me, turning it off with one hand. We were dripping wet.

"What are you doing?" she asked with a little laugh.

"I'm too tired to do this standing, but I need to be inside of you," I said, my voice rough with need.

We tumbled onto the bed. She rolled atop me, wet all over, her knees falling to either side of my hips. I ran my hands over her roughly, cupping her breasts, groaning when her nipples pebbled under my touch. I could feel her slick folds against my cock where she settled over me. She rose up, positioning my cock at her entrance and sank down swiftly. I'd meant to drag this out, to tease her, to make it one she'd remember. Not that I could ever forget any single moment when we were together like this. She didn't let me though.

The moment I was inside of her, I let go. When I was with her like this, I knew I was home, precisely where I needed to be. I surrendered to her, to this magic between us. She set a rhythm, rolling her hips slow and steady, rocking against me. I held onto her, gripping her tight at the hips, feeling her skin give under my fingers. Her hair was a wild wet tangle, her eyes dark with need. Her channel clenched and throbbed around me. Too soon, I was at the edge, not ready to let go yet because I didn't want this moment to end. She leaned forward, dropping kisses along my neck and then making her way to my mouth as her breasts brushed against my chest, the feel of her nipples taut and damp from our shower sliding against me. I reached between us, pressing my thumb against her clit. I felt her tighten and let go, shudders wracking her. She cried out into my mouth, her channel squeezing my cock.

Heat twisted at the base of my spine, and my release roared through me. She drew back slowly, nipping my bottom lip before she straightened. I looked up at her as she sat astride me. I was as close as I could physically be to her. Every so often, I wondered if that would be enough.

"I missed you," she said, her voice husky.

"I missed you too."

My heart pounded strong and steady. I reached up, trailing my fingers along her jaw-line, tracing her lips and taking a deep breath. My heart felt so full I thought it might explode. Then, my stomach growled. Her eyes crinkled at the corners with her smile.

She giggled. "Should we shower again before I go pick up Max and make dinner?"

At my nod, she eased away. I let her take me to the shower and soap me all over again. Later that night, we lay in bed with Max sound asleep in the alcove off to the side of the bedroom. It was late summer with the stars winking in the sky through the skylight. She rolled on her side, resting her hand over my heart.

"I have some news," she said softly.

I idly sifted my fingers through her curls.

"What's that?"

"I'm pregnant."

A wave of emotion rocked me. We hadn't talked about it much, but after she had Max, we had decided to just see what happened. I tried not to think about it much, not wanting to put too much pressure on our hopes and dreams.

"Really?" I asked, angling to look at her.

The moonlight falling through the sky-light cast a silvery glow across her face. I could see the tears glistening in her eyes. I pulled her tight against me, breathing in her scent. I felt her shuddering breath as she nodded against me, her chin bumping my shoulder.

"Uh huh. I took like five pregnancy tests and then I went to see the doctor who thought it was pretty funny that I went there for another test. She pointed out this wasn't our first rodeo and maybe I could relax a little."

I chuckled when she laughed softly. She took another shuddering breath. I slid my palm in a slow pass down her back. I knew this was big for her. Before we'd had Max, she'd worried she wouldn't know how to be a good mother because she had no memories of her mom. Just vague feelings of someone being there. She lifted her head, her eyes catching mine as she reached up to trace my brows.

"Well this is it. You'd better say so now if two is too many," she said softly.

I knew what she was asking even though she didn't voice it specifically.

"I told you. I'm here for the long haul. That means forever. The math doesn't matter."

She dipped her head and dropped a soft kiss on my lips before resting her head against my shoulder. I was still awake when I felt her slip into sleep, her breathing going soft and easy.

Thank you for reading Slow Burn - I hope you loved Maisie & Beck's story!

For more smoking hot firefighter romance, Lucy & Levi's story is up next in Burn So Bad. Get ready to swoon when Levi sets out to win Lucy's heart. "A roller coaster of emotions and chemistry that's off the charts. " Don't miss Levi's story!

Keep reading for a sneak peek!

Be sure to sign up for my newsletter for the latest news, teasers & more! Click here to sign up: http://jhcroixauthor.com/subscribe/

Levi

"Where's Lucy?" I asked.

Amelia Masters sighed. "I just told you. Up..."

Her words were cut off by another voice.

"Oh for God's sake, I'm stuck up here."

I glanced up to see a flash of bright blonde hair just past the corner of the roof.

"Lucy's up there?" Cade Masters asked over my shoulder as he approached us.

"Yes! I'm up here. How hard is this to figure out?" Lucy called from above.

I looked back to Amelia. Lucy Caldwell was her best friend, and they owned and ran Kick A** Construction together. We were at one of their current job sites where they were building a new home.

Cade and I were hotshot firefighters in Willow Brook, Alaska and had volunteered to help when Amelia, Cade's wife, called. It was clear why she'd called Cade directly, rather than the main dispatch number. Lucy sounded pissed. Knowing Lucy the way I did, I'd bet she was beyond annoyed she needed help. She most definitely wouldn't have appreciated an entire crew showing up to handle this.

"Care to explain," Cade said dryly.

"We were working on getting the roof beams in place for the cathedral ceiling. Lucy got trapped up there when one of the beams fell and broke the ladder in half." Amelia paused, her gaze concerned. "I'm guessing she got hurt too because the beam whacked a two-by-four on its way down, and it flipped and hit her. You know Lucy though, she told me to shut up and stop worrying."

"Ah, so that's why you told us to bring a ladder," Cade said, his gaze clearing.

"Yeah, why'd you bring the cherry picker?" she asked in return, glancing over to our vehicle.

Cade and I had collectively decided it would be better to drive the large truck with its extendable arm and bucket if we needed it.

"In case Lucy was hurt," I interjected. "We figured it was better to have this than to try to carry her down a ladder. All you told us was Lucy needed help getting off the scaffolding."

"What the hell are you guys talking about?" Lucy hollered from her perch.

I walked around the corner of the partially constructed home and glanced up. Lucy was perched atop some scaffolding, her blonde hair standing out against the blue sky above.

"How ya doin?" I called.

"I'll be better when one of you gets me down," Lucy replied.

Even from two stories above, she managed to convey her prickly, get-the-hell-away-from-me attitude. From my vantage point, I could see her cradling her arm. I doubted she'd fess up to being injured, so I didn't comment on it. A thread of worry wove through me. I didn't like thinking about her being in pain. Not one bit.

"We'll be up there in just a few," I called up.

I walked back toward Cade. "Let's do this. Better to use the bucket than a ladder."

In short order, Cade was easing me upward in the bucket. Inside of another minute, I was level with where Lucy was.

The moment she saw me, her eyes narrowed and her lips tightened. That bit about Lucy not enjoying anyone's help? Well, she was *not* pleased.

Even with her blond hair a windblown mess, her skin flushed and smudged with dirt, and wearing heavy-duty jeans and a loose t-shirt, she was flat out gorgeous.

"Hey Lucy," I said, my eyes going to her arm.

She'd seated herself on the boards across the top of the scaffolding and slowly straightened, flinching slightly when her arm bumped against one of the metal bars on the scaffolding.

"Your arm okay?" I asked.

Lucy's wide blue eyes swung to me. 'It's fine," she snapped.

I bit back a retort. Normally, I loved to tease Lucy. In fact, the crankier she got, the more I reveled in amping her up. A bit ago, I'd tried to get her to go out with me, but she wouldn't even deign to have dinner with me, so I'd dropped it. That didn't change the fact I wanted her. But I didn't think about that now. Not the time or place. It was quite obvious she was in pain. She could be as cranky as she wanted. I just wanted to get her out of here safely and get her arm taken care of.

"Bring me a little closer," I called down to Cade, eyeing the boards under Lucy's feet and assessing whether it was best for me to lift her from here, or climb out.

Cade carefully adjusted the bucket, bringing it flush against the edge of the scaffolding.

"Perfect," I called to him.

I looked over at Lucy. "How about..."

She stepped to the side of the bucket and started to climb in herself.

"Hey, slow down," I said quickly. "Let me..."

The second I spoke, she lost her balance and reflexively reached to grab the scaffolding with her injured arm. She cried out and lurched, tumbling off the side of the scaffolding. In a flash, I caught her by her other arm.

For a few seconds, the nearly impenetrable get-the-hell-away-from-me expression fell from her face. Her sky blue eyes were wide with fear. I might've been calm—because staying calm in the midst of any kind of emergency was what years of training and working as a hotshot firefighter had taught me—but my heart clenched and worry roared through me.

"I've got you Lucy," I said calmly.

I did. I had a firm grip on her arm. She didn't weigh much. At all. Her attitude belied her size. She was quiet, her eyes locked to my face, before she nodded sharply.

Holding Lucy's gaze, I adjusted my stance and slowly leaned over, hooking my other hand under her armpit. I lifted her up and into the bucket in one swift move. I cradled her against me when I drew her all the way over the side. Once I knew she was safe, I took a slow breath and glanced to her.

"You okay?"

Her eyes flicked away, and she looked at the scaffolding and back to me.

"I guess I should thank you," she said, only the slightest hint of begrudging in her tone.

Leave it to Lucy to be annoyed I'd saved her from falling two stories and possibly killing herself in the process.

"No need to thank me. It's my job," I replied with a wink.

Her eyes narrowed. I didn't know what it was about her, but damn she got to me. It didn't matter that she'd just had a pretty serious brush with danger. Now that her safety was certain, I couldn't help but try to tease her. She kicked her legs, her feet bumping against my thigh.

"Okay, you can put me down now. Consider me rescued," she said with a little laugh.

I hesitated. This was the closest I'd ever gotten to her, and I didn't want to give it up just yet. She thumped her feet against my thigh again.

"Seriously Levi, you can put me down," she insisted, her tone flustered.

I reluctantly eased her down, taking care not to jostle her arm that was quite obviously injured whether she'd admit it or not. Once she was on her feet, I looked over at her as I stepped back.

"No sense in lying. How's your arm?" I asked.

Amelia called up at that moment. "Is Lucy okay?

Lucy sighed and rolled her eyes. "Oh my God. I can talk, you know. I'm fine!"

"Well, don't get all pissy with me," Amelia retorted. "You almost fell from up there. We get to be worried."

I leaned over the side. "She's safe and sound," I called, giving Amelia a thumbs up. "Cade, you wanna bring this thing down now?"

I looked back to Lucy. The bucket jostled slightly as Cade started to lower us.

"So? Your arm?"

She met my eyes with an elaborate sigh. "I think I might've broken it."

For a moment, I forgot this was Lucy, the living, breathing definition of touchy. I stepped to her side and slid my hands down her upper arm, carefully unfolding it. I was moving on reflex. As a hotshot firefighter, I was trained to handle anything and everything, including medical emergencies from minor to major. As my touch traveled along her forearm, I didn't feel a break, but it was already swelling. She was so petite. She barely reached my chin. I could wrap one hand around her wrist with room to spare.

"I'm not feeling a break, but it could be just a crack, or bad bruising. It's swelling along your radius here," I murmured, keeping my touch light as I brushed across the area.

When I glanced up, her gorgeous blue eyes were inches away. My gaze coasted over her face, taking in her fine-boned features—the slight tilt of her nose, her high cheekbones, the delicate arch of her brow, and her full, perfectly bow-shaped pink lips, complete with a dimple in the center of her bottom lip. A streak of dirt on her cheek was endearing, if only because it was so out of place on her face.

My gaze landed on the rapid flutter of her pulse in her neck. My cock twitched, my body tightening in response.

I whipped my eyes back up. This was definitely not the time or place for me to be getting hot over Lucy.

I expected her to shove me away, not that there was much space if she did. Yet, she didn't.

Her mouth twisted with a sigh. "Well, whatever happened, it hurts."

I'd completely lost track of what I'd said for a moment. The feel of her arm resting in my hands nudged me back on track.

"Amelia mentioned she thought a two-by-four hit you."

Lucy nodded. "Yeah, the beam fell and hit the two-by-four on the way down. It whacked me good when it flipped over."

She gave her arm a little tug. "Can I have my arm back?"

I reluctantly let go. Up to these last few moments, Lucy had been a challenge I wanted to beat. Always quick to argue, always turning me down, rarely smiling...and beautiful, so fucking beautiful, she took my breath away.

Conveniently, or not, depending on how you looked at it, the bucket we were in jostled again as Cade brought it to the ground, nudging my attention off of Lucy. Amelia rushed over, just as Lucy started to climb out.

"Are you okay? Oh my God, I can't believe..."

"I'm fine. Can't you see..."

Their words crossed over each other. Meanwhile, I wrapped my hand around Lucy's good arm. "Easy. Let's get you out without jostling that break."

Lucy spun in my direction, her eyes snapping. "I..."

Amelia cut her off. "Don't be silly. Let Levi help you," she ordered.

Amelia was the only woman I knew who might be bossier than Lucy. She was also close to six feet tall and tough as nails. Gorgeous too with her amber hair and eyes, and leggy, curvy build. She was like a sister to me. Good thing because Cade would probably kill any man who took a fancy to her.

He must've gotten out of the truck because he materialized at Amelia's side. I didn't wait to give Lucy any more time to debate how she was getting out. I climbed out swiftly and reached over, lifting her against me.

Her eyes collided with mine. For a flash, it was as if we were alone. With her body bundled up in my arms, she was warm and relaxed against me. The temptation to drag my tongue along the delicate skin along the side of her neck was so great, I had to grit my teeth.

Available now!
Burn So Bad

Be sure to sign up for my newsletter for the latest news, teasers & more! Click here to sign up: http://jhcroixauthor.com/subscribe/

FIND MY BOOKS

Thank you for reading Slow Burn! I hope you enjoyed the story. If so, you can help other readers find my books in a variety of ways.

1) Write a review!
2) Sign up for my newsletter, so you can receive information about upcoming new releases & receive a FREE copy of one of my books: http://jhcroixauthor.com/subscribe/
3) Like and follow my Amazon Author page at https://amazon.com/author/jhcroix
4) Follow me on Bookbub at https://www.bookbub.com/authors/j-h-croix

5) Follow me on Instagram at https://www.
instagram.com/jhcroix/
6) Like my Facebook page at https://www.
facebook.com/jhcroix

———

Into The Fire Series
Burn For Me
Slow Burn
Burn So Bad
Hot Mess
Burn So Good
Sweet Fire
Play With Fire
Melt With You
Burn For You
Crash & Burn
Swoon Series
This Crazy Love
Wait For Me
Break My Fall
Brit Boys Sports Romance
The Play
Big Win
Out Of Bounds
Play Me
Naughty Wish
Diamond Creek Alaska Novels

ACKNOWLEDGMENTS

To my fans: you keep me writing and make every book possible! Many thanks for your input on all the fun stuff, including hot cover models, titles and even town names. No book would make it out to the world without my editor. In that vein, Yoly Cortez makes every cover more amazing than the last and does so with patience and kindness. My proofreaders angels - Terri D., Terri E., Janine, Heather H., Mary & Pat - hugs & kisses for making every book just so.

xoxo

J.H. Croix

ABOUT THE AUTHOR

USA Today Bestselling Author J. H. Croix lives in a small town in the historical farmlands of Maine with her husband and two spoiled dogs. Croix writes contemporary romance with sassy women and alpha men who aren't afraid to show some emotion. Her love for quirky small-towns and the characters that inhabit them shines through in her writing. Take a walk on the wild side of romance with her bestselling novels!

Places you can find me:
jhcroixauthor.com
jhcroix@jhcroix.com

www.ingramcontent.com/pod-product-compliance
Lightning Source LLC
Chambersburg PA
CBHW062016190726
48284CB00012B/261